I0523751

From Enemies to Lovers on Nantucket

Cousins of Nantucket, Volume 2

Taryn Daniels

Published by The Colab Press, 2022.

Chapter One

ELLIE JONES WOULD RATHER shave her head and walk through Nantucket backward than enter the bakery at 4:30 a.m. every morning for the rest of her life. Okay. That was an exaggeration, as her blonde hair was still very much intact on her head. When she owned her own bakery, she was going to hire someone to come at the crack of dawn while she slept in.

Blinking away the last of the blur of sleep, she shuffled into the commercial kitchen and stretched her arms over her head until her shoulders protested. She'd regret not stretching when the time came to knead dough into loaves of bread and rolls. The simplicity of the routine made it easy to fall into a half doze as she poured milk into the stockpot and turned on the heat.

As the milk warmed, she gathered the rest of her ingredients. Flour. Sugar. Yeast . . . Ellie paused when her hand hit the empty shelf where her yeast should be. She blinked. Blinked again, hoping the small container would pop up from nothingness or appear from its hiding place behind the larger jars.

She couldn't make bread for the breakfast customers without yeast. Shoving containers aside, she searched at a frantic pace. The milk would be warm enough soon. If she didn't find the yeast, there would be no fresh bread with breakfast.

This could not be happening. Not today.

It had to be here somewhere. She'd replaced the jar yesterday after making the dinner rolls.

Someone moved it.

That was the only explanation that made sense. She huffed out a breath and planted her hands on her hips. Who would dare mess with her stuff? Her corner of the kitchen was off limits. Everyone knew that. She liked things placed in their proper place.

Even Connor, the main chef, knew better than to move her ingredients. He called it part of her charm. Whatever.

It made baking easier when she knew exactly where to find everything. Who wanted to spend half an hour rummaging through the kitchen looking for yeast when it was supposed to be right here?

Ellie spun in a circle and surveyed the kitchen. No one else had come in yet, leaving her in the vast space alone. She didn't mind the quiet, only the lost sleep. She checked her watch. After five already. She'd plundered the cabinets and walk-in refrigerators longer than she thought. Maybe one more pass through the big pantry.

Nothing.

Forget it. No way she'd find the yeast in time to make bread now. Best she could do was run down to the corner deli when they opened and buy out their supply. Well. She'd found one way to get to sleep in. Lose the yeast.

She turned off the heat before the milk scorched. It would likely be wasted now, but there was no help for it. Ellie moved on to the pie crusts and fillings she needed for the afternoon desserts. No yeast required.

Humming along to the rhythm of cutting butter into the flour, she worked out her frustration with the pastry cutter, slicing it into the mixture until the flour turned crumbly. She added a splash of water and kneaded the dough together before rolling it out onto the counter and reaching for a rolling pin.

The back door opened, letting in a flash of the rising sun and a loud rumble of voices. They mingled together as the breakfast crew stomped in. Ellie kept her attention on the pie crust as she rolled the wooden pin forward. She used her forearms for most of the work to save her hands for the precision work of crimping the edges together.

Connor turned on the radio, and the kitchen filled with the sound of jazz music. "Let's get to work, people." He clapped his hands. Every morning it was the same routine. Connor's little quirk was the same as hers. He enjoyed stability and certainty.

Which begged the question of why she wanted the precarious position of opening her own bakery when most businesses failed within the first year.

Not her.

She slammed a pie tin down on the counter and picked up the pie crust. She wouldn't fail.

"Morning, sunshine." A smooth voice whispered over her right ear.

Ellie screamed and flung the pie crust up as she spun to face the voice. Her palm slammed into the man's face. Pie crust oozed and splattered his cheek, covering his scruffy chin.

He jerked back before her fingers could gouge his eyes.

Laughter erupted from the rest of the kitchen staff. Two of them stood with mouths hanging open while Connor laughed so hard, he paused to wipe tears from his eyes.

Her heart pounded as she recognized the man under the pastry. "Jarrad!" Ellie yanked her hand toward her chest which only served to smear pie crust over her shirt. Should've worn an apron.

He swiped pie crust from his mouth and lobbed it into the trash can. "You could have said good morning like everyone else. Leave it to you to cream me with raw pie crust." Jarrad gathered a glob on the end of his finger. "Is this like cookie dough? Can I eat it?"

"Go ahead." She kept her expression flat, but her insides quivered with the need to laugh. Nothing about the pie crust would hurt him. He'd pranked her enough during their younger years to make this worth every second.

He squinted at her and pressed the ball flat between his thumb and forefinger. "I think I'll pass."

Shoot. She'd hoped he would eat it. The look on his face would be priceless.

Then again, she had no desire to start a prank war with the king of pranks.

Never again.

Ellie scooted around Jarrad and headed toward Connor. "Hey, have you seen my jar of yeast? I couldn't find it this morning, so there's no fresh bread. I'll run down to the deli and pick up what they have."

Connor tied an apron around his waist while shaking his head. "Ask Jarrad. He was the last one in your side of the kitchen yesterday."

"What was he doing in my stuff?" Ellie huffed and crossed her arms. Pie crust smushed between her hand and arm, covering her with goopy stickiness. Great. Now she had dough everywhere. Five minutes with Jarrad had turned her into a walking disaster.

Her stomach still quivered, though she couldn't identify the emotion tied to the flutter. No way she'd attribute the feeling to butterflies in her stomach.

"Ask him." Connor turned away and waved a hand. "I have work to do. Unless you plan on pieing me in the face too?" A split-second flicker passed over his face. It was there and gone before she could identify it. When she shook her head, he shrugged and reached for a stack of skillets he needed to cook the required amount of bacon.

She sent a glance Jarrad's way. He stood at the sink and attempted to scrub the pie dough from his face. Due to the amount of butter she used, he was in for a rude awakening. And some baby-soft skin.

Ellie cracked a grin before Connor's words came back to rest and sent the smile away. He'd been messing with her ingredients. Another prank? If so, she was glad she'd covered him in goop. She stomped to the garbage can and scraped the thick pastry into the trash. Jarrad remained at the sink. Ellie stalked over and shoved her hands under the hot water.

Jarrad squirted dish soap into his hands and scrubbed them over his face. "What's in this? I feel like a greased pig."

"You look like one too."

"Just don't put me on a spit and roast me."

"Oh, but you'd make such a nice compliment to my apple pie." She batted her eyelashes at him. "Tell me what you did with my yeast, and I'll consider letting you off the hook."

"Huh?" He scrubbed and peered at her with one eye. The other closed as soapy water slipped over his nose.

"What did you do with my yeast?" She punctuated each word with a jab of soap-covered fingers to his arm.

"First of all. Ow." He leaned out of reach and splashed water over his face. The force of movement sent water spraying over Ellie.

She spluttered and backed away.

"Sorry." Jarrad flung his head back, sending waves of brown hair flopping back and then forward, almost obscuring his eyes.

Ellie clenched her hands and the soap squelched. Oh, right. She still needed to rinse her hands.

While Jarrad dried his face, she rinsed off and reached for a second towel. One of the many good things about an industrial kitchen, clean towels everywhere.

Connor shouted out an order for bacon and eggs, and the kitchen burst into movement. Bacon sizzled. The scent made Ellie's stomach rumble with hunger.

Jarrad started to move away. Ellie grabbed his arm and pulled him around to face her. "Not so fast."

"I really have no idea what you're talking about, Ellie. What yeast?"

She jammed a finger in his chest. "You were in my stuff yesterday. Connor saw you. Second shelf. Small red container. What did you do with it?"

Jarrad rubbed the spot where she poked him and frowned. "I threw it away."

"What? Why?"

"It was empty."

They were toe-to-toe now, their breaths mingling. Jarrad locked eyes with her, his blue and soft and without guile. For now. His gaze roved her face, pausing at her lips. He pulled in a breath the pushed his chest closer. The hand that had been rubbing his chest moved toward her cheek, making it halfway before he dropped it to his side.

"Are you pranking me right now? Because it wasn't empty. I put it on the shelf after refilling it. Where it should have stayed because everyone knows to leave my ingredients alone." Every breath brought them closer together. A tingle of awareness began in her stomach and worked its way outward. She couldn't back down. Ellie fought against the pull.

Eyes widening, Jarrad ran a hand over his mouth and around to his neck. He squeezed and released. "I'm sorry, Ellie. I didn't know. I saw it on the counter earlier in the day and it was empty. I just assumed . . ."

He trailed off. She filled in the gaps. He'd assumed the container was still empty and tossed it in the trash.

She took a step back. "Fine. Say I believe you. Stay out of my stuff." She backed up another step. Jarrad followed her with his gaze, and her heart kicked up an extra beat. She needed to get out of here. "Connor, I'm going to the deli to get bread."

He waved a spatula to show he'd heard and bellowed another order. Ellie escaped out the back door and tugged off a glob of stuck-on pastry.

What was that?

Jarrad was the enemy. He worked the afternoon shift. They should not be crossing paths at breakfast.

JARRAD MOVED TO HIS station as the door slammed behind Ellie. He'd messed up. Big time. The flare in her eyes said she wouldn't forget anytime soon.

Connor flipped several pieces of bacon and looked up when Jarrad moved to the stove next to the main cook. "I wouldn't want to be you right now." He shook his head. "Not that I've ever wanted to be you. But that thing between you and Ellie just now—" He whistled. "—not good."

He could say that again. Jarrad kept his mouth shut and got to work on the side dishes needed for the morning. Hash browns and the occasional fried egg. Those were his only responsibilities right now until Connor started to trust him with more.

He'd thought Ellie had forgotten all those childhood pranks. Her reaction today said otherwise. She looked ready to roll him in dough and bake him into a pie. That look was one of his favorites. When she pushed her shoulders back and one hand went to her narrow hip, he felt like the men in those chick flicks who lost their breath at the sight of the woman they eventually fell in love with.

Jarrad spooned butter into a skillet and waited on the sizzle before dropping in an egg. *Focus on work, you dolt.* He needed this job. And the morning shift was light years better than the afternoons he'd been working.

Ellie flew back into the kitchen.

He barely held in a comment asking where she'd hidden the broom she rode in on. That one would get him banned for life. Not what he wanted.

"I thought you worked the afternoon shift." Ellie glared at him from across the room, which grew silent save the scrape of spatulas and the sizzle of frying food.

Everyone in the kitchen seemed to hold their breath. One of the women even leaned forward like she wanted closer to the action. Kitchen gossip spread faster than butter on a hot skillet. And was harder to contain. Anything overheard here was fair game to be spread over Nantucket by the time the sun sank over the horizon tonight.

"Connor let me switch." He kept to the facts and avoided the personal reasons he wanted the mornings. His parents offered to let him clean the unit they owned at Rose Resort. The resort Ellie's parents managed. The second income might be enough to support him. If he was careful.

Questions darted across her face, but none made it past her lips. Jarrad lifted the perfectly cooked egg onto a plate and handed it to Connor. They continued down the line, filling order after order. Ellie fumed and tapped her toes. "Don't you have work to do?" He said it with a lilt of laughter in his voice, but Ellie puffed up her chest and stomped away.

Minutes later, she returned with a small machine in her hands. She jabbed the buttons, ripped something from the top, and slapped it onto the row of cabinets where he'd found the jar of yeast. A label maker? Seriously. The woman was labeling her cabinets like he was the type to be put off by a sticker.

An idea struck hard and fast, as all his best pranks did. He could move all the labels. Sticking them on random objects. Like the toilet. He needed to see what she was typing out. Nodding at Connor, Jarrad slid around the stove and up to the row where Ellie pressed another white strip of paper onto the smooth chrome cabinet. ELLIE'S STUFF.

Oh man. She'd just handed him the mother of all pranks.

An oven door squeaked, and the scent of warm biscuits filled the kitchen. Ellie turned to face the sound and found Jarrad blocking her path. She scrambled back a step, bumping her backside on the handle to the walk-in freezer. She grimaced and shifted the other way.

He had her trapped.

"You did good work with that dough in my face. I'll be looking to pay you back. Maybe."

"Maybe?" Her eyes widened, the blue depths rivaling the ocean. Strands of blonde hair drifted over her shoulders, the curls growing wild in the heat of the kitchen. He'd seen them in every state over the years. From perfectly contained ringlets to this, where it looked like she'd rolled out of bed and not even bothered to run a brush through her hair. *Stay away from that train of thought.*

The question hovered between them, as thick as the steam puffing from a locomotive. Attraction came with it. A desire to see Ellie's eyes light up with the mischief he remembered.

He'd pranked her to get her attention, but she never realized it. The only attention he garnered was the kind where she either screamed at him or ran away crying. He never understood why.

Things could be different now.

Ellie lifted the label maker like it was Captain America's shield. "I need to get this back to the office."

He stepped to the side and let her pass. When she reached his side, he leaned over and whispered, "You have pie dough stuck to your chin."

"Why didn't you tell me that before I walked halfway across town?" Pink bloomed across her cheeks.

Shoot. He'd done it again.

Chapter Two

HOW COULD A PERSON be this tired at noon? Ellie yawned and blinked to clear her vision. She double-checked the numbers in the column, comparing them to the receipt in her hand. Thank goodness they matched. The last thing she wanted to do was repeat the last hour of copying numbers into the books for her parents.

She liked the job well enough except for these moments when fatigue threatened to hold her eyelids shut despite the sunshine beaming straight down outside.

The soft click-clack of her mom's stride came from the door behind Ellie. She straightened her shoulders and lifted her chin to keep the lines of exhaustion from showing.

"Ellie honey, I need you to take off the cleaning bill for unit 12. We won't be charging them this month." Her mother's steps halted, and her cucumber coconut lotion filled the surrounding area.

Unit 12. The Olson unit. Jarrad's parents had owned the space for as long as Ellie could remember. She stopped her work and looked up. Mom's blonde hair was swept to the side, the fringe of bangs perfectly framing and drawing attention to her blue eyes. Every year, Ellie heard how much she looked like her mom. As a teenager, she'd been skeptical. Now she hoped it was true. Her mom was a knockout.

"Are the Olsons not staying this year?" Ellie drummed her fingers on the desk. It wouldn't be the first time the couple stayed on the mainland, but with Jarrad on Nantucket, she'd assumed his parents wouldn't be far behind.

Mom reached down and squeezed Ellie's shoulder. "They've made arrangements for Jarrad to clean for them. They'll pay him instead of us billing for a cleaning service."

That was . . . unusual. Why would the Olsons pay their son to clean? They had more money than anyone Ellie knew. Jarrad was the spoiled rich kid who tormented everyone.

Now he was working two jobs? Neither of which paid big bucks. What was he up to?

"Why?" Ellie spun the swivel chair around until she faced her mother. "Why would Jarrad do that?"

"If you think that's crazy, wait till you hear this. I've also agreed to let him clean unit 16 before the Smiths check in." Her mom's smile was not the least bit forced. She looked . . . happy. Happy that she was helping Jarrad?

"Mom. Check in is in two hours. Jarrad has never cleaned before. We can't guarantee his work. Someone will have to check up on him before the Smiths arrive and ensure the unit is immaculate."

"Don't worry about that. We'll bill his parents for the cleaning service if everything isn't perfect."

Ellie gripped the desk. "I can't believe you'd trust him after what he did." Ellie's voice started to rise. She slammed her lips shut and gripped the pencil until her knuckles began to ache. Her fingertips tingled when she released the pressure.

Mom sat in the chair beside Ellie and reached for her hand. "Honey, are you talking about the time he stole your bra and hung it on the sign?"

Yes. The memory washed over Ellie. She'd been a young teen and not yet fully developed. Back then, she'd worn push-up bras to help fill everything out and help her not feel self-conscious. Jarrad slipped into her room and stole her favorite bra. It was bright red and had a row of lace at the top that made her feel feminine and pretty. He'd hung it on the resort sign right at the edge of town, for everyone on Nantucket to see.

She'd been mortified. To make matters worse, he'd scrawled her name across the cups, so everyone knew it belonged to her.

"That was the worst day of my life, Mom."

"I remember. You didn't even want to go to school." Mom hugged Ellie tight. "But we don't know that he's the one responsible. No one saw him take it, and he never owned up to the prank. Your father almost approached the Olsons and demanded an apology, but without proof, there was nothing he could do."

"That wasn't a prank. Putting salt in someone's tea is a prank. That was—" Ellie fluttered her hands. "I don't even have words for how atrocious that was. Life-altering. Excruciating. I wanted to leave Nantucket and never show my face again." Which was a big deal for someone who was born and raised here. Her entire family were true residents, not the vacationers or part-timers who claimed the island as home but spent half the year on the mainland.

This was home, and Jarrad ruined it.

"I don't trust him."

"I'm sorry, but the deal is done."

Her jaw ached from the pressure of holding back her anger. "What if he messes up?"

Mom's sigh was long and said she'd reached the end of her patience with Ellie. "Then I'll talk to his parents, and we'll go back to how things were. They know this is on a trial basis. We've been friends long enough they won't mind if I tell them it isn't working."

Ellie swallowed another angry retort. Mom was right. The Olsons and the Jones went way back. Years and years. Even before Ellie and Jarrad were born. She saw Jarrad every summer for years when his family came in. They could have been friends if he'd had a shred of respect for others and how his pranks made them feel.

Reality crashed down on Ellie. Not only would she face Jarrad at the restaurant in the mornings, but now she'd be forced to see him in the afternoons when he came to clean, and she worked the books.

There was no way to avoid him, especially since she planned on checking up on his cleaning skills. She refused to let the resort's reputation suffer because of Jarrad. Her parents worked too hard to build the place into what it was now.

They expected perfection from all their staff. Ellie included. Daughter or not, she'd worked here every day since her teenage years on a pitiful wage that most would turn up their nose at. She'd considered walking away, but the family ties were too strong. What she didn't earn in money, she gained in a strong work ethic and the ability to see her parents live a life they loved.

She did insist on buying her own house away from the resort, though. Much as she loved her parents, she needed her own independence and room to breathe without them looking over her shoulder like her mother was doing now.

Ellie felt the pressure on the back of her neck as her mom scanned the books for errors.

What if Jarrad decided to restart his pranks? His maybe from this morning echoed in her head. She did not want to relive those days of looking over her shoulder. The instant she knew Jarrad was on the island, it all came back. The fear and uncertainty. The impulse to check under her bed and between the covers to make sure he'd not left a centipede or other nasty for her to discover in the middle of the night.

She had to make sure it didn't happen. If it took a month of fake smiles and pretend cheer to keep the pranks at bay, so be it. She could fake happiness at working with Jarrad. No one said she had to talk to him, but she could be professional. She worked with problem clients all the time and never once lost her temper. Jarrad would be a testament to her ability to adapt. A test run of her patience and practice for working with people she might not like when running her bakery.

As though conjured by the mere mention of the pranks he'd pulled, Jarrad strolled into the lobby. Dressed in cargo shorts and a worn t-shirt the color of the ocean, he crossed the room in a few long strides and dropped his forearms onto the top of the reception desk. The move put

Ellie at a disadvantage as she sat in the chair. She popped up and dislodged her mom's arms from around her shoulders.

WHOA. Jarrad did his best not to gape at Ellie. When she jumped up, the pink sundress caressing her curves and her hair curling around her face, he'd understood how Jim Carrey felt in *The Mask* when he saw Cameron Diaz on stage and his heart beat out of his chest.

His own heart attempted a feeble recovery, but his racing pulse begged for attention.

Ellie smoothed her hands over her stomach. Did she feel butterflies? Isn't that what all the girls went on about? Saying they felt butterflies in their stomach when someone they were attracted to came near?

He hoped so. When he took the cleaning job, it was to help pad his pockets while getting out from his dad's real estate business, but he admitted that the chance to see Ellie every day was an extra incentive. Maybe even the main attraction.

"Jarrad, you're right on time." Mrs. Jones stood and swept her hand toward Ellie. "Ellie will show you around. You'll need supplies from the main closet before you head to the unit."

"Yes, ma'am." Jarrad inclined his head in a short nod but kept his gaze on Ellie. She seemed to be working through something. Her eyes were bright, but she chewed on the inside of her cheek, causing the muscle there to clench and release.

Hmmm. What made Ellie Jones tick?

She came to some sort of consensus and moved around the desk. "Right this way." She strode ahead of him, giving him a view of her shoulders and back. And more, if he chose to look.

Nope. He was a mature adult, not some ogler.

His palms began to sweat as Ellie led him down a hallway, past the kitchen, and toward a wooden door with SUPPLIES etched on a chrome plate screwed in at eye level.

Ellie pried a key from behind the plate and shoved it into the doorknob. "Sometimes the door sticks. If that happens, push on it here"—she shoved her hip into the middle of the door—"and it should open right up." The door screeched as it grated across the floor.

"You know, it wouldn't take five minutes to fix that." He ran a finger along the back of the door where the hinges attached. "Looks like a hinge has bent and is letting the door tilt, making it catch on the floor."

Ellie's eyebrows shot upward, and her hands gripped her hips. "Well then, Mr-fix-it, why don't you put that on your duty list."

"I will." He sauntered into the closet and surveyed the shelves. Cleaning supplies. Rags. All the usual stuff.

"Vacuums, brooms, and mops are in each unit, but you'll find everything else here." Ellie's voice had a pleasant lilt to it. It was as though she'd forgotten all about their morning shenanigans with missing yeast.

She could be the next Vanna White with the way she moved around the small space, pointing out all the different types of cleaners and what they were for.

"This floor cleaner says multi-purpose, but never, ever use it on anything other than the floors." She tapped a brown bottle and waited for him to acknowledge her before she moved on. "Trash pickup is on Monday and Thursday. Make sure the beds have been changed and the refrigerator emptied before you leave. And check the microwave. People forget stuff in there all the time and it starts stinking. We once had a tenant leave a salad in there and the next renters had quite the surprise when they opened the microwave to heat a cup of coffee." Her nose wrinkled and caused tiny lines to fan out around her eyes.

Stunning. Ellie Jones had grown into a gorgeous woman. When he first saw her at the restaurant before her cousin's wedding, he'd noticed her bubbly personality. Like champagne, she popped and fizzed and made his insides tingle. Then she blasted him in the restaurant this morning and he saw her sassy side, which he could freely admit—to himself—he admired.

This Ellie was all polite business and gentle hospitality. No wonder the guests loved her.

Which was the real Ellie, or were they all part of the whole and she picked each personality based on the moment?

"What happens if I come across a clogged toilet?" *Seriously? You couldn't come up with anything better than that?*

"Plungers are under the sink in the unit. Figure it out." A flash of sassy Ellie emerged with her wry grin and innocent eyes.

This had potential. Who needed serious every minute of every day? That mentality was part of what drove him back to Nantucket, where life moved a little slower, a little more carefree, and the weight of adulthood didn't stifle him like the sweaters his Nana knit every year.

"What kind of problems do I call you for?"

"This is not Ghostbusters. I'm not who you're gonna call." Ellie wiggled her fingers at him.

Laughter filled his chest and rang out before he could rein it in. He'd not expected her sarcasm. "Aw, come on. You can be Janine and I'll be Egon." He tested her knowledge of the original and was rewarded with a smirk.

"If you're anyone, you're Venkman. You have the prankster part down to a science."

Hmm. She had a point. "You know your *Ghostbusters*."

"What can I say, Dad loves movies that make him nostalgic."

Ouch. What did it mean that no one forced him to watch the 80s and 90s movies? He loved the corny jokes and story lines. This was good, though. They had something in common. He could talk old movies and test the waters to see where Ellie stood with him. She seemed warmer today, more open.

He gathered up a handful of supplies and shoved them into one of the plastic caddies that held everything in one spot and had an easy to grip handle. "Well then, Princess Buttercup, I'm off to clean the stables."

She shook her head, but a real smile stretched across her face. "You'll never be a Wesley."

"As you wish." He bowed at the waist and backed from the room. Best to leave while he'd reached a point where she didn't glare at him or act like he was something to be scraped from the bottom of her shoe.

Progress.

Jarrad whistled while making his way down the stone path. Unit 16 was close enough to his parents' unit 12 that he could see the corner of the building as he opened the door and stepped inside. He'd clean 16 first since the couple would be arriving in a few hours, then move to his parents' space. His mom demanded he send photos when he finished before she would send his money.

Not that she didn't trust him, but after he'd failed so many times by letting the renters pass their inspections, she had reasons to doubt him. He froze two steps into the living room. Was this payback for refusing to make the renters go through multiple inspections? His sister had a knack for finding any little thing wrong and forcing the renters to pay more money as they required inspection after inspection. Surely his mom wouldn't do that.

Or would she?

Cold dread gripped his chest. He shoved it aside. He'd worry about all that later. He had a guaranteed payment with this unit and a short amount of time to make a good impression.

A need to impress Ellie dropped into his gut and hardened. He could to it. He could be polite and act like a grown up. Which meant putting aside the pranks, even though Ellie's reactions begged him to dive back into that world. No. No more Venkman. He would become Egon to her Janine. Serious. Astute. Problem-solver and world-saver extraordinaire. And as long as a giant marshmallow didn't come to life and threaten to destroy Nantucket, he might get the chance to ask Ellie out on a date.

If they developed into more, well, he wouldn't complain. And if it proved to his dad that Jarrad knew how to adult, then he'd have made his point. He didn't need the stress and confines of his dad's stuffy real estate company.

Chapter Three

ELLIE WAS BECOMING one of those women who survived the day thanks to coffee. She sipped her extra large latte with three espresso shots and felt every drop of caffeine jar her system awake. It was Friday afternoon for crying out loud and she was exhausted. Instead of feeling giddy and planning a trip to the beach, she was curled in her comfy chair cradling the latte like it held the secret to the fountain of youth.

Being around Jarrad every day frazzled her nerves and made her jumpier than a cricket. *Don't think about bugs.* She shuddered and pulled her feet further under the fuzzy blanket draped over her lap. It took her an hour of searching her bedroom last night before she could fall asleep feeling secure in the knowledge that Jarrad hadn't slipped into her room and left a nasty surprise.

They were adults, it was time he started acting like it.

She gulped the hot liquid. He'd been cordial this week. Downright agreeable. She didn't trust it. He was luring her in like a spider to its web.

Her phone rang, and she jumped, sloshing coffee across her chest. She answered with a groan and fanned her shirt to cool her skin.

"Get dressed. We're going out."

Ellie checked the screen. Only one person ordered her around like that, but just to be sure, she verified the name at the top of the screen. "Samantha, I don't feel like going anywhere."

"Which is exactly why I'm parked in your driveway. You need a break." The sound of a door opening came through the phone, followed by a door slamming outside Ellie's house. "I'm coming in." Samantha ended the call.

Well. That's ominous. Ellie didn't move. Samantha could let herself into the house.

She followed her cousin's progress through each sound. The rattle of the knob on the front door. Samantha's brief pounding knock. The scrape of the flower planter being shoved aside as Samantha searched for the spare key. Finally, the lock clicked and the door opened. Samantha closed it with a solid bang. "You can't hide from me."

"Wouldn't dream of it." Ellie muttered into her mug. Her damp shirt clung to her chest, chilling her skin. She rose and moved to the closet.

Samantha strolled into the bedroom. "Good. You're changing. I was afraid I'd have to tie you up and play country music until you begged for mercy and agreed to go out."

"You wouldn't dare."

"I would." Samantha crossed her arms and lifted her chin. "You need to get out and live life."

"I need a nap and another latte." And a bakery where she was in charge of scheduling. Ellie faced the mirror. Dark circles and puffy eyes. Pale skin. Samantha might be right. She needed to get out. Her social life was non-existent and had been since she started working at the restaurant. Working two jobs that kept her running from before daylight until after sundown would wear on anyone, even a mid-twenties woman like herself.

Samantha didn't move. She kept staring at Ellie in the mirror and gave a nod when she sighed. "I knew you'd end up seeing it my way. Honestly, why do you do this to yourself?"

"Because I'm an upstanding daughter who learned at a young age to work hard for what I want even when the pay sucks?"

"Yeah, okay. I'll let you have that one. But what are you going to do when you have your bakery? Will you still work for your parents?" The look on Samantha's face said she thought Ellie was crazy for sticking it out this long.

Her parents really did win the day when Ellie finally grew old enough to start working. They paid her pennies on the dollar compared to what a non-family employee would cost. It took her ten years to get up the nerve to ask for a raise. Even then, they acted like she'd requested the moon.

She had her own house—that she paid rent on like a normal adult—and never asked for anything from her parents. They were not fans of kids who assumed they were owed something simply because they existed. Which made her curious why they were so willing to help Jarrad out when the man clearly had money. He wore the name brand clothes and the popular shoes that cost more than she made in a week. Maybe even a month. Jarrad and job went together about as well as anchovies and sour kraut.

"What's that look?" Samantha moved her finger around in a circle near Ellie's face. "You look like you just realized ice cream isn't calorie free."

Don't say Jarrad. Ellie closed her eyes and scrambled for something to say that wouldn't betray her inner feelings. Then again. She opened her eyes and looked back at Samantha. Maybe a chat with her bestie cousin would help clear the air and put her head back on straight. She took a breath. "Mom and Dad hired Jarrad to clean in the afternoons."

Samantha's lips twitched. She clapped a hand over her mouth, but a giggle slipped out.

"This isn't funny." Ellie threw the shirt at Sam's face.

Sam swatted it away. "Yeah. It kind of is. You two are the perfect couple."

"Right." Ellie snorted. "If by couple you mean two people who hate each other."

"He doesn't hate you. And I'm pretty sure you don't hate him." Samantha threw the shirt back, and Ellie caught it with one hand. "Now, get dressed. Come bake on the beach. We're going to relax, eat great food, and have a chat about boys."

Boys. Ha! She had it partly right. Jarrad didn't act like a grown man. Well. Maybe sometimes. They did manage to work an entire week together without him pulling any pranks.

"He definitely grew into his looks." Samantha fiddled with her hoop earring and searched Ellie's face.

Another good point. Jarrad grew up physically in his time away. Broad shoulders. Gorgeous brown hair that fell in natural waves and left a little long on top, so it fell over his forehead when he leaned forward. Nice lips and a face no longer covered in zits. Yep. He'd matured on the outside.

It was the inside that concerned Ellie.

Samantha grinned widely and plopped onto the bed. "You like him."

Ellie still held the shirt, and she twisted it around in her hands. If she didn't stop, it would be a tangled mess and she'd need to find a different shirt. But she liked this one. The off-the-shoulder cut showed off her arms and back in a way that made her feel feminine and pretty. She retreated to the bathroom while waving her hand at Samantha. "I don't like him. I tolerate him because we work together. He's way too immature for me."

"Because you're so old and decrepit." Samantha's tone said everything Ellie needed to hear. Her cousin didn't believe her. Too bad. She meant it. Jarrad Olson was the pesky teenager who never grew up. He was like Peter Pan without the lost boys or Wendy or Tinkerbell to teach him how to navigate life as an adult. "You're being a little unfair, don't you think?" Sam's voice moved closer to the door. "I saw how he looked at you at the restaurant when we celebrated Katrina's wedding. The man was smitten."

"Whatever." Ellie huffed and changed into the white shirt. It caught on her chin and sent her in a circle as she attempted to tug it over her stomach while removing it from her face. "I'm not looking for a relationship. Bakery first and most important priority. Remember?"

Shirt in place, she ran her favorite lip gloss over her lips and refreshed her mascara. After twelve hours between the restaurant and the resort, she needed a full overhaul, but the sun would be going down soon, and no one would notice the bags under her eyes.

No one cared enough to look for them or be concerned except Samantha. Katrina if she wasn't still on her honeymoon being ridiculously happy. Ellie didn't envy her . . . much.

Samantha rapped on the door. "Let's go. You're beautiful. Stop fidgeting."

"Bossy." Ellie muttered before stepping out of the bathroom.

"If I didn't fuss, you'd never get out. You complain at least once a month about not having a social life. This is me, making sure you don't wither up into a prune. You're a butterfly. Go, flap those beautiful wings."

"You're ridiculous." But she felt better knowing Samantha pushed her to have these rare moments with her friends outside of work. They were few and far between, but oh so necessary. She might regret it in the morning when the alarm rang. Scratch that. She *would* regret it. Her cozy chair beckoned, the yellow blanket promising warmth and relaxation.

Samantha hooked her arm around Ellie's and pulled her to the front door. "Outside." She paused long enough to let Ellie lock the door before angling them toward the beach a short hike from the house.

Ellie breathed deeply and lifted her face to the waning light. A sigh caught in her chest. She'd missed this. Nantucket was one of those places that she never thought she'd take for granted. With its long beaches begging for bare feet and the epic sunrises and sunsets, Nantucket had nestled itself in her heart and soul. Like so many who lived here, she sometimes forgot that the rest of the world came here to experience a slice of their perfect island while the residents stood by and shook their heads.

She stepped onto the wooden walkway and caught sight of the sand on the other end. Her steps grew quicker, enticing a laugh from Sam, who stepped back and let Ellie race ahead. At the last step, she kicked off her sandals and stuck her feet in the sand.

Perfectly coarse and warm from the day, she sank into the grainy texture until her feet disappeared. "I've missed this." Her thoughts slipped out at the same time a deep chuckle rumbled from the side. Her heart gave a traitorous leap. She knew that laugh. Was it cosmic betrayal that put Jarrad on the same beach at the same time?

It felt like betrayal. Or a setup. Ellie cracked her eyes open in a squint and turned to glare at Samantha. "Did you do this?"

"By this, you mean ask Jarrad to be here?" She shook her head, but laughter filled her eyes and her teeth flashed with her wide smile. "Wasn't me."

"He better not come over here." Ellie ground her molars.

Samantha snorted. "Too late. He's walking this way. Want me to scare him off?"

"Yes. No. Maybe." Ellie drew the salt air into her lungs and let it soothe her frayed nerves. She could do this. Calm. Professional. Casual. No reason to let him know how he affected her and that he was partly to blame for the circles around her eyes. She took another fortifying breath, and this one brought the scent of fresh lobster smothered in butter. Her mouth watered and her feet moved of their own accord toward the delicious scent.

Jarrad stood in the middle of a group. His back was to her, giving her a view of his lean legs. He wore board shorts and nothing else. Ellie let her gaze roam. As long as he didn't catch her staring, she could enjoy the moment. Her cheeks flushed. Muscles rippled across Jarrad's back when he lifted a hand and waved as a second group approached from the other end of the beach.

He started to turn Ellie's way. She spun and headed toward the water, perpendicular to the group.

"I think he felt you looking at him. That stare was next level." Sam skipped alongside Ellie. If no one knew better, they'd think Sam was the one with the perky personality that was usually attributed to Ellie.

"You brought up how good he looked. I needed to access before I could validate your statement."

"Whatever." Sam's laughter rang out, loud and long, causing half the group to turn their way.

Jarrad waved and shouted something, his words swallowed up by the crash of waves that churned across the beach and washed over Ellie's feet. Samantha waved back, saving Ellie the trouble.

"Let's get some food." Sam urged Ellie toward the fire and their friends. Jarrad excluded.

She wasn't being fair. She didn't feel like being fair. Not after their history. But she did her best to put a pleasant smile on her face and relax her body, so she didn't appear tense.

Jarrad passed her a plate, which she passed to Samantha, and then she took a plate from Leslie, one of the hostesses at the restaurant. Leslie smiled and leaned closer to Ellie. She waited for the woman to say something, but she seemed more interested in getting closer to Jarrad than anything.

More power to her. Ellie stepped back and around and smiled at Leslie. Taking the hint, Leslie slid into Ellie's spot and struck up a conversation with Jarrad.

Ellie watched the crowd swell as another group arrived. Connor raced across the sand and slid to a stop beside her. "Hey."

"Hey." Man. When was the last time she saw Connor outside of work? He cleaned up nice. Even his aftershave was different, spicier. She liked it. "Some party." She dipped her lobster tail in the butter and brought the bite to her lips.

Connor licked his lips and blushed. Maybe it was the heat of the fire blazing at Ellie's back. The heat was intense and forced her to take a step away. Laughter filled the air, a mixture of voices and pitches that created a melody of joy.

Ellie faced the ocean and waited for the sun to touch the water. Her favorite moment approached. That second when a breath of air separated the sun and the ocean and it appeared to hover, begging for a touch.

"You look nice tonight." Connor spoke from beside her.

Ellie turned and missed the first graze of the sunset. Her stomach churned. Was he flirting? No way. Not Connor. They worked together. Same as she worked with Jarrad. They had a work relationship.

She mumbled a thanks and ate another bite to save herself from talking.

Samantha ran over. "We're dancing. Come on." She took Ellie's plate and handed it to Connor. "Hold that. Please."

Before Ellie could protest, music joined the laughter. It was loud and fast. Just what she needed to jar her caffeine-fueled system into overdrive. The sounds of guitar and piano ran the length of her spine and put her in motion. She hooked arms with Samantha and spun in a circle. Her laughter refused to be contained and it burst from her lips without apology.

She threw her arms up to the sky and stomped her feet. Leslie and Jarrad picked up the beat. Sand flew in every direction. Ellie spun again. A hand caught her waist and twirled her out before bringing her back in. She slammed into Jarrad's chest, her hand landing over his heart. A rapid thump fluttered beneath her fingertips. His smile was long and slow, changing as the music changed. The hand at her waist tightened and brought her closer to Jarrad's body until they were close enough that she saw beads of sweat in his hairline and smelled the sharp sweetness of his cologne.

The music swelled and soared into the night. Jarrad brought her around until the sunset came into view. He rocked side to side. Not dancing so much as shuffling. Did she dare let her cheek rest on his shoulder? The urge persisted despite every argument she threw at it.

They were wrong for each other. She had no desire to do this with Jarrad. He couldn't be trusted.

"Hey, Ellie, did you bring any desserts?" The random question brought Ellie out of her comatose state. She pushed her way out of Jarrad's embrace. Desserts. Bakery. Those were her goals. Falling in love, no way.

Even if she fit in his arms and he made her want to curl up like a cat and purr her contentment.

Priorities, Ellie.

"Sorry. No desserts. Maybe next time." She started to walk away.

Jarrad reached out a hand as though to stop her. Ellie backed up, and he dropped the offending appendage. "Thanks for the dance." She took another step and bumped into someone. "Sorry."

"No problem." Connor braced her back with his arm.

Jarrad frowned and his gaze moved from Ellie to Connor's hand on her hip. A muscle ticked in his forearm, and he was clenching and unclenching his hand.

She had no idea what that meant, but her face went hot, and her skin prickled with goosebumps. Connor let go when she moved to the side. "I think I'll go home."

"You want me to walk you?" Both men spoke, their words tumbling over each other like the tide washing over the same spot time and again until it wore the sand away.

"No thanks." She directed the answer over her shoulder as she escaped.

And if her pulse pounded, she blamed it on the exertion of jogging up the steps and down the dock. She slowed when she reached the path and felt her way through the darkness until she reached her house with her cozy chair and fuzzy blanket.

Chapter Four

THE BEST PART ABOUT strolling into the kitchen at 6 a.m. was seeing Ellie. If not for that incentive, Jarrad might have turned off the alarm and went back to sleep. Today he'd been especially tempted to throw the covers over his head.

Instead, he joined the others as they streamed into the kitchen and destroyed the peace and quiet. Ellie didn't move from her station or react to the racket.

Jarrad moved closer, slinking her way slower than an inch worm on an apple tree. If he could surprise her again, he'd probably take another slap of dough to the face. And it would be worth it. Before he made it to her, Connor jumped between them and called Ellie's name. She lifted her head, angling it at Connor, and removed a set of earbuds. No wonder she didn't hear them enter.

"Quick meeting before we get started." Connor rubbed his hands together.

Jarrad didn't like the smile on the cook's face. He looked too exuberant for this time in the morning.

Ellie turned and caught sight of him. Her gaze slid away, leaving him with a solid knot in his gut. Could she not bear to even look at him anymore? Why? He'd not done anything.

"I need everyone's attention." Connor clapped his hands and the kitchen staff converged into a loose semi-circle around their leader.

Jarrad waited toward the back as Ellie washed her hands before joining them.

Connor surveyed the crowd and locked his attention on Ellie. "We have a conference group coming on Wednesday. It was a last-minute booking, and it's going to cause a time crunch. They'll be holding meetings in the ballroom until Saturday. This is a big one. Major corporation and they're an eco-friendly group, so watch yourselves. Ellie, I need you to prepare a range of pastries, each with a gluten-free option. They have requested a vegan lunch that I'll be overseeing. We must have our full attention on this, people. Dietary restrictions are to be handled with the utmost care. Treat this as though one slip up might cause anaphylactic shock. I want everyone on their A-game."

Ellie nodded and started to chew on her lip. No doubt already planning the three-day menu in her head. She'd need help with the work.

Connor seemed to read his mind. "Considering the time crunch and the amount of food to prepare, I need two people to help Ellie."

"I'll do it." Jarrad threw his hand into the air before Connor could name someone else. After the way things went down at the clambake a few nights ago, he had a suspicion that Connor had set his eyes on Ellie. Not happening.

A grimace tightened Connor's lips, but he nodded. "Fine. Jarrad, you and Becky are with Ellie. The rest of you will maintain your regular duties but be prepared to pitch in if someone asks."

"But—" Ellie started to argue, but Connor was already dismissing the group.

"Put me to work, boss." Jarrad rubbed his palms together. He could get used to this. Connor never let him do anything but fry eggs.

Ellie closed her eyes and took a deep breath. When she opened them, she looked disappointed. "So it's not a dream."

Ouch. Was he that hard to work with? He'd show her what Jarrad Olson was made of. "Come on, Ellie. We can do this. I'll be the best helper you've ever had."

"No pranks." She held up her pointer finger, then waved it side to side. "If I even *think* you're trying to prank me, you're out, back on stove duty."

He held up his hands in surrender. "No pranks. Got it."

"I mean it. This is important, not just for me but for the entire business. The Club Car Restaurant should present itself as the epitome of sophistication."

She was taking this a bit too seriously, but whatever. He could handle it. After all, how hard could it be to make a bunch of desserts?

An hour later, he realized what he'd gotten himself into. Ellie turned from sweet and innocent to drill sergeant at the snap of her fingers. She ordered Becky to start over on the gluten-free pie crust when the first one kept tearing when she moved it to the pie tin.

Jarrad stirred the batch of pie filling and hid a grin under the guise of wiping his face with a towel. He'd followed the directions on Ellie's recipe card, and the aroma of apples and spice made his mouth water. Surely he could try a bite. Quality control and all that. He reached for a spoon and scooped an apple up to his mouth.

"What are you doing?" Ellie clapped her hands onto her hips and glared at him. She took the spoon away and dropped the bite back into the pot, where it simmered along with its delicious counterparts. He'd assume they were delicious since Ellie continued to stare at him. "Do you know what it's supposed to taste like?"

"Pie." Wasn't that what he was making? Apple pie. Didn't take a rocket scientist to figure out it should taste like apples. There were a dozen in the pot. He knew. He'd peeled and diced every last one. Flavor profile complete.

Ellie rocked her head from side to side and clicked her tongue. "You have no idea. You just want to eat it. And if you eat it, there won't be any for the conference. Then I get in trouble for not being able to control my staff. Then I get a reputation for being a push over and when I open my own bakery, no one will respect me as a boss."

"What now? How did we get from apples to you being the owner of a bakery?" He kept stirring. Who knew what she'd do if he deviated from the recipe that specifically stated—in bold and highlighted—stir constantly for twenty minutes while mixture thickens?

Ellie flushed. "Don't worry about that. Just do your job. Follow the recipe. If it says sample the product, then go ahead." She smirked and folded her arms. "But it won't. You know how I know? Because I wrote all the recipes."

She was enjoying this. Maybe too much. He liked a good challenge, and Ellie presented him with his best one yet. He'd promised no pranks, but this didn't count. He motioned at the pot. "Could you take over for a minute?"

Her eyes narrowed. "Why?"

"Are you allowed to ask me that? Aren't I allowed a break after an hour of following your every demand?" He kept his tone innocent and let go of the spoon.

Ellie took it and turned her back to him. "Five minutes."

He only needed one.

Jarrad ran through the kitchen and into the office, where he grabbed a pencil from the desk and ran back to the table where Ellie's recipe cards lay strewn around. He picked up the next card she had laid out for him and scribbled a tiny note at the bottom. When he returned to the stove, she handed him the spoon and left without a word or a backward glance.

Becky looked up from her pie crust and smiled at him. "Don't let it bother you. Ellie gets carried away sometimes, but she's never mean."

"She really opening her own bakery?"

Becky shrugged. "I mean, I guess so. She doesn't really talk about it." She picked up the crust and swiveled to place it in the pie tin. A breath puffed her cheeks when it transferred without a hitch.

The squeak of an oven door turned Jarrad around. Ellie checked on her cookies, her lips puckered as she tapped her chin. She pulled the tray out, sending the zing of lemon into the air.

"What are those?"

"Lemon shortbread cookies." Ellie's curls danced over her shoulders. She gave them an impatient shove and reached for a hairnet. Not the most stylish look, but one the kitchen required. Every few seconds, she gave the cookies a poke with her finger. A frown pulled at her lips.

Jarrad checked the timer. Five minutes of stirring left. Suddenly he was grateful for his workouts giving him the strength to go round and round with a wooden spoon for twenty minutes. How pitiful would it look if this simple act wore him out. He'd be the laughing stock of the kitchen.

None of that mattered right now, though, as Ellie tried to lift a cookie and it crumbled in her hands.

"Argh!" She slapped the counter with her palm. "The almond flour isn't working. Becky, can you get the rice flour from the pantry?"

Becky checked her watch and nodded. "Pie crust needs two more minutes. I have time."

"Thanks." Ellie called out to Becky's retreating back.

"Should you be testing new recipes with this much pressure on you already?" He meant for the question to help Ellie realize she might be asking too much of herself.

From the way her shoulders jerked back, she took it as a challenge. Her words confirmed it. "You think I don't have what it takes to pull this off?"

"Whoa." He held up his free hand, the other never stopping its round and round motion. "You're more than capable. I meant you don't have to make up a bunch of new stuff for this conference. If you had a month, sure, perfect new recipes. But you have a day, at most, before we're against the wire." He couldn't believe he was saying it. He, Jarrad Olson, the risk-taker and fly-by-the-seat-of-your-pants man was telling someone to stick to the well-known. What made it funny was that he was trying to convince the most routine-driven person he'd ever known.

Why the sudden change?

JARRAD WAS MAKING SENSE. Why was Jarrad making sense?

Ellie pushed away from the tray of cookies and focused. She'd been waiting to test out the recipe, knowing it would need perfecting. Why did she want it ready in two days?

Easy. Because she wanted to impress the group. If they came back next year, she'd have her bakery open. Having a company seek her out for her delicacies and sweets would elevate the business. They'd go home and talk about the delicious cookies to their friends, who would look her up. If they couldn't come to Nantucket, maybe she could send the flavors of Nantucket to them. If she packaged them right, cookies could easily be flown to the mainland. Other businesses did it all the time.

"Ellie?" Jarrad's face swam before her, the lines of his chin drawing clearer as she blinked.

He stood on the other side of the counter with his palms on the clean surface and a question on his lips. *Do not think about his lips.* Too late. Ellie pulled her thoughts into order. This could be her big chance, but she needed to find a way to impress without risking a catastrophic failure. "Lavender. Where's the lavender scone recipe?"

Jarrad's brows furrowed, and he lifted his hands to his apron pocket. "Right here. I'm starting them next."

She held out her hand. "Let me do this one. I have an idea. You get started on Choux pastry dough. We can store it in pastry bags in the refrigerator until we need it Wednesday." Was she really going to let him work on one of the harder doughs? Yes. She swallowed her doubts. The mixing was not the hard part. It was the baking where Choux dough became finicky. She'd handle that part herself.

He hesitated long enough to make her nerve endings tingle. And what was that look in his eye. "Jarrad?"

"I was trying to help you relax." He pulled the card out and passed it over.

On the bottom, written in a hasty scrawl, she read aloud, "Jarrad taste tests the final product." She should be irritated. He'd broken the rule and messed with her stuff. Though the card wasn't labeled, he knew it was hers. He'd deliberately done this. Laughter worked its way up from behind her naval and bubbled in her throat. "Are you that desperate for food? Doesn't anyone feed you?"

He grinned and the sounds of the kitchen bled away for a heart-stopping moment, leaving them encased in a bubble where his smile made her knees turn wobbly.

Smoke billowed from Becky's oven and a shrill alarm blared. Jarrad burst into action, turning the oven off and pulling out the blackened crust. Becky returned from the pantry with the bag of rice flour in her arms. "Sorry it took me so long. I couldn't find . . ." She trailed off, dropped the bag onto the counter, and ran to Jarrad's side. "My crust. What happened? I had the timer set. I know I did." She pushed ingredients aside and reached for the timer. Her groan matched the look on Jarrad's face. "Two hours. I set it for two hours, not two minutes. I'm sorry, Ellie."

This week was going to be a disaster. A headache pulsed behind her eyes and her throat constricted around a lump. If this was what it was like to run a bakery . . . No. She refused to think like that. Mistakes happened. Things like this were bound to come up. How she reacted was what mattered. She could get angry and scream and shout, but it wouldn't change anything.

Ellie threw an arm around Becky's shoulders. "It's okay."

Connor silenced the smoke detector and stepped out front to reassure everyone that the kitchen was fine and the food unharmed.

Becky's eyes welled with tears. "I'm sorry."

"Don't worry about it. These things happen." She squeezed the slim shoulder. "Don't let it get you down. We still have plenty of time. Why don't you get started on another crust?"

Becky nodded and dried her eyes. "Thanks for understanding." She walked away, her smile once more in place.

Jarrad cut Ellie off before she could retreat to her station. "You took that really well."

"You sound surprised."

"Well."

When he didn't continue, Ellie crossed her arms. "I'm not that hard to work with."

"So it's just me you don't like." He said it flatly, turning it into a statement.

Her next breath caught somewhere between her lungs and her esophagus, stopping the words she needed to say. One second passed, then another. Jarrad stared without blinking, and she knew he wouldn't move or return to work until they resolved whatever this was between them. Ellie forced her lungs to cooperate with an inhale. She took his arm and pulled him toward the walk-in pantry at the back of the kitchen. Only after she closed the door did she speak. "This has nothing to do with liking you. We have history. You played so many pranks on me that I don't know how to trust you. But I'm willing to try, because this job is important. I need you to do your part. No pranks. Just work. Do that and maybe I can learn to trust you."

He leaned close. The scent of his cologne imprinted itself on her mind. She'd never smell it without thinking of him. He reached out and took a bar of chocolate from the shelf. "I swear on this chocolate bar that I will do nothing to sabotage your work. I will uphold the highest integrity and honor as bestowed upon me by the depth of my love for dessert."

"That makes no sense, but I accept your promise." Ellie rested her hand on top of the chocolate. Her fingertips touched his wrist, sending a shock up her arm. His skin was warm and smooth, his pulse beating beneath her index finger.

"I won't let you down." There was a seriousness in his eyes that she'd never seen before. This was not the prankster of her youth. This was a man certain of what he wanted.

The chocolate pressed between their palms.

"Has anyone seen the lima beans?" Connor shoved the door open and froze. He looked at Jarrad and then Ellie. A crease appeared between his eyes. "Everything okay in here?" His tone grew colder with each word. "Find something you like?"

Jarrad slid his hand from Ellie's. "Needed a quick sugar fix." He waved the chocolate. "I was going to eat this."

"But then I reminded him that those are unsweetened." Ellie snatched a banana from the basket at her elbow and pushed it at Jarrad's chest. "You should eat this instead. Better for you."

"Hey, chocolate comes from a plant."

Ellie bit back the burst of laughter. "Don't even try it. Eat the chocolate if you want. I promise you'll regret it." Jarrad still didn't look convinced. "Have you ever eaten a spoonful of cocoa?" He nodded. "That's worse. Think of it as compressed cocoa. One bite equal to several spoonfuls. It's disgusting on its own."

"But delicious when combined with sugar and butter and eggs." His eyes shined. "Brownies. You should make gourmet brownies for the conference. They're a cinch to convert to gluten-free."

Ellie grabbed Jarrad's face and kissed his forehead before her mind could catch up to her actions. "You're a genius." She let go and scrambled back a step, her face growing hot. "I need my recipes."

Both men remained in place as though they'd been turned to stone. Ellie ran, her heart thumping painfully behind her ribs. What had she just done?

Chapter Five

JARRAD PACED THE STRETCH of packed sand and waited for Nathan. He checked his watch. Five minutes late. He'd give the man another five minutes because he was Ellie's brother. After catching up with Nathan after Katrina's wedding, they'd tried a couple times to meet up for a run but nothing ever worked out. Jarrad didn't mind running solo, but a chance to talk to Nathan was what he needed right now. He'd have insights into Ellie, if he was willing to share about his sister.

"Hey, sorry I'm late. Detention." Nathan jogged over and slapped a hand to Jarrad's shoulder.

Jarrad snickered. "Thought you got out of detention once you graduated."

"If only." Nathan shook his head. "This one kid is determined to push me over the edge. Yesterday he tried to snap a girl's bra strap while she walked down the hallway. Major blowup with the parents."

"And all he got was detention?"

"Oh, we have a few punishments for him." Nathan lifted his knees toward his chest and twisted his shoulders. "Ready?"

Jarrad did a hamstring stretch before he nodded. "Let's go."

They hit that perfect place where the tide brushed the sand and packed it down, allowing them to run without sinking. The sand still tugged at Jarrad's feet, and his calves burned after a few strides.

"You back on Nantucket for good?" Nathan asked between pants.

Good. Jarrad wasn't the only one struggling. No marathons for him anytime soon. "Hope so." And he did. If this all worked out, he'd become a permanent resident instead of the kid who showed up every summer and stuck around long enough to form attachments that left him longing for more but never able to commit. Between the job at the Club Car and cleaning at Rose Resort, he was managing to make ends meet. The thing with Ellie stumped him. What was with that kiss in the pantry this morning?

There'd been no time to move or react. A fact he regretted now.

"How's Ellie?" Nathan wiped a hand over his face but kept his eyes forward.

"You probably know better than me." That was the truth. Other than helping her, he hadn't seen her. Even when he stood in the kitchen right beside Ellie, she was too focused on her food to pay attention to him. It made him itchy with a need to do something to gain her focus. He wanted her to look his way and see him. Really see him and how hard he was trying to make up for hurting her.

He still didn't understand why his pranks made her react the way they did, but he could see the effects all these years later. Her lack of faith and trust in him hurt.

They ran in silence for the next mile. Nathan slowed first, his breath wheezing with each inhale. "I need a favor."

Jarrad stretched and waited. He didn't have enough air in his lungs for much more than single word answers anyway.

"Look out for Ellie." Concern pinched Nathan's eyes.

Most people couldn't tell the Jones twins apart. They were identical down to the way they moved. But Nathan's expressions gave him away. Where Tim showed nothing but concern for himself and how to get ahead in life, Nathan had a genuine gift for wanting what was best for others. Mainly his sister.

"Why does she need looking after?"

"She doesn't." Nathan grinned and Jarrad saw a flash of Tim in the look. "It was more of a warning. I love my sister. Mess with her and I'll make you regret it."

Not what he'd expected to hear this afternoon. Did Nathan know about the kiss? What would he do if he knew Jarrad had feelings for

Ellie? He opened his mouth to ask, then clamped it shut. No need in pushing something that might amount to nothing. He had a mountain to overcome before Ellie would consider him worth her time.

All the money his family had didn't matter to a woman like her. She'd proved that over the years. Until she could take a plate of food from him and eat it without checking every morsel or passing over it altogether, he didn't have a leg to stand on.

His alarm rang a warning. Time to head over to the resort for cleaning duty. He said goodbye to Nathan and retreated to the shady paths that would lead him anywhere on the island.

Maybe he'd run into Ellie tonight. Though, from the way he smelled, he hoped not. From now on, he'd run earlier and shower before dropping by her parents' resort. So far, Mrs. Jones had no complaints about his cleaning and his parents had upheld their end of the bargain. He sent pictures each day, assuring them he was keeping the place spotless, and his payments had arrived without fail.

"Jarrad, wait."

He spun toward the sound of his name. Connor approached. The look on his face had Jarrad holding his breath as he waited for bad news to spew from the man's mouth. A look like that only came with bad news.

"I need you on the afternoon shift."

"Tonight? But I worked this morning, and I'm supposed to help Ellie prepare for the conference. She only has one more day before they arrive."

Connor scowled. "And I say I need you on the afternoon shift. I'll help Ellie."

"Who'll do your job then?" Jarrad crossed his arms. He didn't like this. Something about Connor didn't sit right. Why agree this morning only to change his mind hours later? A memory of Connor's face at the clambake and again in the pantry flashed through Jarrad. "You like Ellie. You're trying to get me out of the way so you can ask her out."

"We work together. I don't date my employees. It sets a bad example." But he took a step back as though surprised. "You've been following her around, distracting her from her work. I've seen how you look at her."

And he'd seen Ellie kiss Jarrad. On the forehead. Still. It counted.

"Nothing wrong with looking." Jarrad pushed the advantage. "Why move me? I'm useless on the afternoon shift. All I do is bus tables. I'm a help to Ellie, and that's where I want to stay."

"Well, you don't have a say in the matter." Connor turned on his heel. "Be there at seven tonight or don't bother coming back at all. And just so you know, Ellie gets carried away sometimes and kisses people. Don't think that moment in the pantry was anything special. She kissed me a while back on a dare." And it was probably the best moment of his life and the reason Connor wanted Jarrad out of the way.

That's how he wanted to play it, fine. Jarrad knew this method of posturing and chest-puffing. He'd played before.

Right this minute, though, he had a job to do before returning to the restaurant. Jarrad broke into a sprint and raced to Rose Resort. He slowed to a walk before entering the lobby and crossed his fingers that Ellie wouldn't be sitting at the desk.

The cosmos laughed at him. Ellie wasn't behind the desk but in front of it. With her arms crossed. "You're late."

What was with Nantucket today? Was the entire island out to get him?

"Couldn't be helped." He panted the words with his hands on his knees. Every inhale burned, but the exhales scorched all the way up. "Water." He took a shaky step toward the water cooler with its ridiculous little paper cups. He'd need twenty to ease the pain in his throat.

"We have a policy of timeliness and cleanliness." Ellie gave a cautious sniff in his direction. "You're failing both today?"

Jarrad gulped the first cup down in a single swallow. "Is this about our kiss in the pantry? Are you trying to punish me for your feelings?"

Ellie's cheeks reddened. "I don't have feelings for you."

"I don't believe you." He kept his tone light and teasing.

Ellie locked her jaw and turned away. "You won't get another warning." She stomped away.

Welcome to your date with Karma. First Nathan, then Connor, now Ellie. He'd heard bad things come in threes but nothing like this. It felt like the universe wanted him to leave Ellie alone. Good thing he knew how to ignore unwanted advice.

He would like to know what caused Ellie's sudden retreat. Sure the kiss in the pantry was platonic, but he'd seen the blush on her cheeks then and again now. She wouldn't blush like that unless she felt something for him, right?

THE NEXT MORNING, ELLIE took an extra minute to prepare herself before the morning crew walked in. She'd been unbearably mean to Jarrad yesterday. All because her attraction to him frightened her. He was unreliable and bound to leave Nantucket once he grew bored with playing at middle class. She tightened her armor around her heart as the door opened.

Connor entered first and made his way to her side. "I'm all yours today. Tell me what to do."

"Where's Jarrad?" At her question, Connor's jaw twitched.

He cleared his throat. "Jarrad is working the afternoon shift."

Because of her? Had he requested the change? Ellie didn't have the courage to ask or the time to worry about Jarrad when she had twenty-four hours to prepare for the twenty-person conference. She handed Connor a list. "Start there. Let me know when you're finished with each task. I'll need to check it before you move on to the next job."

"You want to check my work?"

Surely he wasn't surprised. Ellie regarded Connor's expression before she answered. Eyebrows up. Mouth down. Hands clenching the paper. "Would you turn me loose on a stove and let me send out food without checking it?"

"No."

"Same goes for me. It's my reputation on the line if anything in the desserts go wrong. I need perfection." Her palms grew damp and she swiped them on her apron. Connor knew how to cook. But could he bake? They were not the same, regardless of how many people considered baking the easier of the two, there was an art to the things she created. Same with Connor's creations. Equally important yet distinct in their differences. "Follow the list." She took a step back.

"I won't disappoint you." She recognized the promise in his words. Connor believed in his work. He'd do his best, no matter what the job entailed. He moved to Jarrad's station and retrieved the stack of stainless steel bowls from the shelf before moving to turn the radio on.

Soft jazz eased the nervous energy building inside Ellie's chest. She could do this. Success here meant success for her bakery.

Working with Connor was easy. He seemed to anticipate what she needed and had it ready for her before she could ask. While she worked pie crust, he brought a stack of pie tins. When she moved to put the crusts in the oven, he took the dirty dishes to the sink. Every task on his list, he completed with a level of skill she expected of his expertise and precision in the kitchen.

After the first few hours, she grew confident in his ability to do as she asked and stopped checking in on him.

She moved on to the Choux dough fillings. Chocolate first, then a nice lemon curd. She wanted the flavor of Cannoli but in a bite-sized morsel.

Connor scooted to her side while holding one of her recipe cards. Her heart didn't jump at his approach, but a warmth enveloped her chest. No pranks. No jump scares. Being with Connor let her be comfortable and relaxed. She needed this, not the constant jumble of emotions Jarrad caused.

"There's some leftover potato soup from last night's service. Why don't you take a break?" Connor flicked the card with his finger. "I'll work on this."

She considered arguing but the rumble in her belly ended the idea. "Why don't you join me? We're ahead of schedule, and you haven't had a break all morning." Unlike Jarrad who thrived on disappearing for five minutes when she needed him most. *Not fair, Ellie.* Why did she keep putting Jarrad down? Was it such a deep-seated reflex at this point that it happened automatically?

"I'll get the soup. Do you want bread?" Connor moved toward the pantry.

Ellie snapped her fingers. "Brilliant idea. Let's make bread bowls."

Connor's grin made crescents appear in his cheeks. "Now we're talking." He motioned at the rows of fresh bread she'd baked before he arrived. "I'll heat the soup while you pick the bread. You know more about it than me."

And he owned up to his weaknesses too. Ellie hummed to herself while scooping out the soft center of two large dinner rolls. The crusty outside would hold the soup while the heat and liquid turned the hard edges soft and doughy. Perfection. She put the empty crusts on separate plates and Connor ladled steaming soup inside. Not everyone enjoyed a fall-inspired soup when the temperature outside hit eighty, but she loved it.

They didn't get snow on Nantucket, so she took the chance to enjoy the hearty potatoes with hints of cheddar and bacon. She dunked a piece of bread into the broth and popped it into her mouth. A sigh slipped out.

"Good?" Connor watched her while scooping each bite into his mouth after scraping the bottom of the spoon across the lip of the bread bowl. He didn't spill a single drop.

Ellie had a trail of golden deliciousness across her plate and felt at least one drop hit her chin. "I've never had potato soup this good."

"It's my grandmother's recipe." Connor blushed but didn't shift away. "She's never shared it before, but I talked her into it. She made me promise I'd never tell a soul. I'm not even allowed to write down the recipe. If I forget it, that's it."

"She wouldn't give it to you again?"

"No way. The only way I learned it was to watch and help her make it until I got it right. She wouldn't let me write it down, and I haven't, even to this day. It's a family heirloom." He chuckled and wiped his mouth.

Ellie shredded her bowl, the once firm bread now a yielding participant in the destruction as it came apart in layers that begged to be eaten.

Connor didn't touch his bread except to put pieces on his spoon, stir them into the soup, then fish them out again in single bites. She considered herself particular, but Connor bypassed her. He chewed each bite thoroughly before swallowing and wiped his mouth every single time.

The traits that made him a perfectionist in the kitchen seemed to shift to his daily life as well.

Ellie didn't mind. She'd bet his kitchen floor was clean enough to eat from. Not that she'd offer to test the theory.

What about Jarrad? She didn't even know where he was staying, much less what kind of housekeeping he'd keep up with. He'd managed to do the cleaning at the resort without complaint. Mom and Dad were happy with his work. Ellie feared they let things slide because of who Jarrad was. She ought to check on his unit. To ensure the job was done right and to their high standards.

"What's next?" Connor cleaned the few crumbs from his plate and tossed his bread in the trash.

Ellie used the last lump of bread to swipe up any remaining soup before answering. "I'm going to finish this batch of filling then call it a day. Everything else needs to be made tomorrow morning. If we bake too early, it'll be dry when the attendees arrive. No one like dry desserts." She brushed her hands off and moved her dirty dishes to the sink where Betsy was busy scrubbing a stack of plates. Ellie nodded her thanks and washed her hands.

"I'll double-check the pantry and refrigerator. Make sure everything on your list is done." Connor paused as though to say something else. His mouth pinched, but then he shook his head and smiled. "I'll be here in the morning to help."

"You don't have to do that." Really, she didn't want him interrupting her early morning vibe, but she couldn't say that, not to her boss. Especially when he'd been so helpful today. "I have it under control."

"I insist. As you said, it's your reputation on the line. Mine too." He strolled away but stopped at the next stove to check Louis' temperatures on a burger about to go out. He shook his head and pointed at the grill. Louis dropped the patty back onto the grill and waited for Connor to give the okay.

He had strict rules about food, and the kitchen ran better for them. Ellie needed to remember that when she opened her bakery. He never put anyone down, but he held firm and was willing to teach. Good management made for good employees.

Ellie mentally ticked off a box on her check list. Treat employees like they matter, and they'll want to stick around. She would miss this place.

Chapter Six

WEDNESDAY MORNING CAME with a flurry of activity in the kitchen. Ellie piped chocolate filling into the last of the Choux dough and straightened her spine. The muscles and tendons screamed over her release from their hunched position. She'd done it. Two hundred orbs of dough, baked perfectly and filled with deliciousness. She handed the platter to Becky. "Add those to the rest."

Connor hurried around the kitchen, barking orders and shaking his head at the smallest infraction. He'd been forced to abandon Ellie this morning and take over the brigade.

The conference attendees had arrived an hour early, putting the head chef in a tailspin as he attempted to push everyone to do the impossible.

Becky turned, holding the tray close to her chest.

Connor waved a hand as Becky walked by. Ellie lunged as time slowed. Connor's hand brushed the edge of the tray, hardly more than a bump, but it was enough to upset Becky's hold. The platter tilted.

Becky's eyes grew round. She attempted to recover at the same time Connor spun and reached for her hands. Their combined efforts sent the Choux straight up into the air. Ellie shuttered her eyes against the wink of hours of hard work being tossed up like a clown juggling a hundred balls at once.

A squeak of protest slid past her lips, but it was too late.

The desserts hit the ground with audible pops. Several of them burst open, spilling chocolate across the floor.

Everyone froze and pulled in a collective breath. Silence reigned over the kitchen. Even the food cooking in myriad skillets grew quiet as though to mourn the disaster. The staff turned their attention to Ellie, waiting for her reaction.

"Ellie—"

She held up a hand to stop Connor. If she spoke, she'd regret it later. The words running through her head were hard and cold and unnecessary. Things like this happened in a kitchen. *All that matters is how you react to it.* Ellie lifted her shoulders and forced a smile. She tipped her chin in acknowledgment of Connor's muttered "sorry" and headed to the pantry to gather up ingredients for a new batch.

A frenzy of activity filled the kitchen once more with sound. Becky ran behind Ellie and snatched the chocolate from the shelf. "I'll do the chocolate filling."

"I'll get the lemon curd started." Connor poked his head into the kitchen. His lips were compressed in a thin line, but there was a resolute look in his eyes that Ellie didn't feel like arguing with.

She missed Jarrad. The thought slammed home and knocked her back a step. If Jarrad was here, he'd have found a way to make her smile. The knot in her throat would disappear and she'd smile. Without his goofiness, she felt off kilter and tense. A disaster waiting to happen.

Ellie took a breath and closed her eyes, letting the hum of the kitchen fill her. She could do this. One disaster did not mean the entire week would follow the same path. One moment at a time. All she needed to do was make Choux pastry.

She'd made it a hundred times.

Nothing about this day made the recipe any different.

Becky left the pantry, the swish of the door announcing her departure.

Ellie kept her eyes closed and breathed in, holding the scent of chocolate and pastry close to her heart before letting it all out and forcing the anxiousness from her muscles.

When she left the pantry, no one paid her any mind. They all had their own jobs to do, regardless of Ellie's problem.

She wouldn't fail.

Ingredients lined up on the counter like little soldiers preparing for war, Ellie began.

Hours later, another platter of delicacies waited where before there were only individual ingredients.

This was her favorite part, seeing potential turn into product. Her hands trembled as Connor took the platter and added it to the others on the other side of the kitchen.

He came to her side and touched her elbow. "Go home. Relax for a while. We have another big day tomorrow and you've put in overtime already."

Ellie checked her watch. Three p.m. She was late to the resort. "Thanks for all your help."

"My pleasure." He gave her a look that said he meant every word.

Her cheeks flushed but she didn't answer. Taking off her apron and tossing it in the basket, she smoothed her hair and ran out the door. Mom would understand, but that didn't make it okay.

She burst into the Rose Resort out of breath and with hair flying around her face to find Mom, Dad, and Jarrad sitting behind the desk in what appeared to be a serious discussion. He looked up at her approach and his lips quirked up at the corners. "You're just in time."

Dad stood and looped an arm around Ellie's waist. "Hello, sweetheart." His white hair curled over his ears. Line fanned out from his eyes. Eyes filled with laughter and a hint of mischief.

They were up to something. She had no idea what, but it was in the air as clear as the storm brewing on the horizon in the painting behind her mother's head. Her stomach churned like those storm clouds. "What's going on?"

"Jarrad is fixing the supply room door. He needs your help." Mom stood and planted a hand on her hip. "Your father would help, but he's promised to take me to the Club Car for dinner for our anniversary."

Ellie groaned and smacked her forehead. "I forgot your anniversary. I'm sorry." She hugged her dad, then Mom. "Happy anniversary."

"Thank you." Dad patted her back. "Nathan is going to cover the front while you help Jarrad."

"Wait. Why doesn't Nathan help Jarrad while I run the front?" It made more sense to her that the two men worked in the back. She had no idea how to fix a door with a bad hinge or whatever it was Jarrad said was wrong. Nathan would be more help in that department.

Mom shook her head. "Nathan needs the practice with the computer. We only have one couple checking in this evening. It'll be nice and slow so he can handle that. I need you to make sure the cleaning supplies are put back where they belong and no one gets into the closet while Jarrad has the door."

"What about his cleaning duties. Shouldn't he do them first?"

"Already finished." Jarrad grinned at her, a full-blown smile that made her insides do that fluttery thing. "You can check my work if you don't believe me."

And spend more time with him than was necessary? No thanks. But then, why did it feel like disappointment rattled deep down inside?

"Nathan will be here—"

"Right now." Her brother interrupted Dad and strode toward the desk where he clapped Dad on the back after hugging Mom. "Sorry I haven't been by more often. School's crazy right now."

"Any more detentions?" Jarrad asked from his seated position. He'd not moved since Ellie walked in except to get comfortable in her favorite chair.

Detention?

Nathan laughed. "No. Thank goodness. I think he learned his lesson."

Jarrad and Nathan were friends? The idea was surreal. Ellie took a step back. "Well, if no one needs me, I'm going to run into the kitchen."

She needed a drink of water. Or a snack. Or to wake up from this dream.

Surely that's what this was. It couldn't be her real life. Her parents, her brother, they hadn't accepted Jarrad into the resort like he was family. Any minute now she'd wake up and find out it was all a nightmare.

Jarrad popped up. "I'll come with you. I could use a bottle of water before we get started."

Ellie waited for Nathan to protest, but he smiled at her and continued a conversation with Mom and Dad about checking in their guests later.

If she didn't know better, she'd accuse them of setting her up and forcing her to work with Jarrad. Why would they? The animosity she felt for him hadn't interfered. Had it?

That was ridiculous.

"How'd it go this morning?"

I missed you. Ellie froze those words and forced them down. "Fine. Had to remake all your Choux pastry."

They moved into the kitchen, a smaller version of the restaurant's but better suited to their needs here at the Rose Resort.

"What? Why? It was perfect."

"Yeah, it was." She paused and waited for Jarrad to look at her. "Until Connor bumped the tray from Becky's hands, and they all hit the floor."

"Ouch. Tough break. That why you're late today?" Jarrad winced and rubbed the back of his neck.

"You know my schedule?"

"Yes. Why? Is it weird?"

She took two bottles of water from the refrigerator and passed him one. "Little bit."

"You're worth paying attention to." The plastic bottle crinkled in Jarrad's hand. He chugged half the bottle before looking at Ellie again.

She couldn't breathe or even think after that little quip. Did he mean it?

He tapped his bottle to hers. "We should get to work."

Without answering, Ellie followed him down the hallway. If her teenage self could see her now. Helping Jarrad and receiving compliments all in the same day. Definitely a dream. Though maybe not a nightmare as she first suspected.

JARRAD OPENED THE SUPPLY closet door and winced as the screech grated on his ear drums.

Ellie clapped her hands over her ears. "It's gotten worse."

"Which is why I insisted on fixing it today." He'd put his plan into action as soon as he arrived for cleaning. It was his one afternoon off from the restaurant and he had nothing else to occupy his time. Why not spend an extra few minutes with Ellie? He could stretch this job out to an hour, maybe two, if he played things right. She'd never know, and he could continue laying the groundwork to prove he'd matured since they were kids.

Connor taking him from morning duty threw a wrench in Jarrad's progress. He had to think fast to get back on track. Connor obviously had his own sights set on Ellie, whether she realized it or not.

Ellie tucked herself against a shelf and crossed her arms. "There's really no reason for me to be here. I'll be in your way."

Never. But he couldn't say that. "The Roberts have a three-year-old who's been out roaming the halls once already. I need you to make sure he doesn't get in here while I have the door off."

"Nathan could do that."

"Am I that hard to work with?" He genuinely needed to know. Winning her over was one thing, but if she hated him desperately then he'd be better off moving on. He pulled a Phillips screwdriver from his pocket and worked on turning the screws on the hinges. The squeak of metal twisting in the wood sounded loud in Ellie's silence. Jarrad waited.

Finally, a soft sigh reached his ears. "No. Much as it pains me to admit, you're easy to work with. You follow directions and you know how to read a recipe."

"My instructor will be thrilled. Can I get you to write that down and send it to him? I have his email address." He'd loved the classes, but man, some of the instructors had zero sense of humor. He hadn't meant to set fire to the creme brulee. Twice.

How was he to know that burnt sugar didn't mean scorch it until it turned dark as the sky at midnight?

"Instructor?" Ellie squeaked and her steps brought her to his elbow. "You went to college?"

"Culinary classes. Last year. Thought it would be fun to be a chef."

"And?"

The first screw dropped into his palm, followed by the second. Jarrad paused before starting on the third and faced Ellie. "And I found a knack for cooking. I graduated top of my class."

Ellie put her fingertips to her mouth. "So why are you working as a busboy?"

Because Connor felt threatened. Or so Jarrad's pride insisted. "Still not sure if I want to cook or manage a kitchen. Cooking's more fun. I've been looking for a building to turn into my own restaurant." He let the words dangle.

"Me too." Both palms landed over her mouth and pink colored Ellie's cheeks. "Please." She dropped her hands. "Don't tell Connor. I don't . . . I don't know for sure that I'll leave and open my own bakery. He shouldn't worry about something that isn't certain. Especially with the stress of this week already drowning us."

Us. He was no longer included in that us, and he despised it. It should have been him working with her this morning. Then maybe she wouldn't have shown up at the resort looking like she'd been through a tsunami.

He returned to the door. "I'll keep your secret if you'll keep mine." He felt more than saw her nod.

Minutes of silence passed. When he started on the final screw, Ellie spoke. "Why are you doing all this? Working at the restaurant. Working here. I thought you worked for your parents."

"Turns out I'm not cut out for real estate." He grunted as the door started to press against his shoulder.

Ellie put a hand on the door and held it away from him. "What did you do there?"

What hadn't he done? Bitter laughter filled his throat. "Nothing I was good at. Apparently, I'm too soft on the renters and I'm no good at sales. Too honest." That was putting it mildly. Not once did he make his quota of sales. He wanted the new owners to know what they were getting. He made sure the building inspections were honest and listed every fault, which made him a favorite with the people looking to rent or buy. Not so much with his dad.

After getting taken off the sales team, he'd been demoted to inspections, where he failed even more spectacularly.

"So you know contracts? What to look for in a building." There was a thoughtful tilt to Ellie's voice.

Of course. She needed a building too. This was his chance. He took out the last screw and stood to take the door from Ellie's grip. "If you ever need my help, I'm all yours. Inspections. Contracts. I can walk you through every step. Be happy to help." He meant every word. Had never meant anything more.

Ellie swallowed hard and let go of the door. She brushed her hands together and took a step back. "You're nothing like what I expected."

"Good." He longed to move closer but couldn't risk the door falling. "I'm nothing like that kid you remember."

"I think I believe you."

Five little words never sounded so sweet. Trust. Belief. He'd prove himself worthy yet. His dad might not think he had a snowball's chance of making something of himself. He'd prove them all wrong. This was where he belonged. On Nantucket with the people who made him feel like he mattered.

Here, he could be Jarrad, chef and entrepreneur, instead of falling under his dad's shadow, unable to be himself.

Sliding the door to the side, he went to work on the hinges. The old ones were bend and rusty. It was a wonder they'd lasted this long. Any kind of metal had to be watched when you lived this close to salt water. Corrosion crept in little by little. If it wasn't watched, then everything fell apart.

"Tell me about your business. Desserts, right?" She was too good at sweet treats to pass up the opportunity to bake full time.

Ellie's head bobbed in a twitchy nod. She glanced at him, then down at the door. "Pastries mostly. Maybe a few breakfast foods. Scones. Cannoli. I'm not set on a menu yet. I thought I'd better find a location first, then worry about the type of food. I don't think I'm ready yet."

"I see your reasoning there." He fitted the new hinges and kept his gaze on his work. Looking at Ellie too long muddied his thoughts. "I'll keep my eyes open for a place. Don't sell yourself short. You're a great baker. Best I've ever known." He looked up and smiled, enjoying the way her eyes widened and her lips parted. A desire to kiss her rose. Not yet. She'd run if he kissed her now.

Chapter Seven

THURSDAY AND FRIDAY passed without incident, but left Ellie drained and too exhausted to roll herself over much less answer her ringing phone on Saturday morning. The second time it rang until the voicemail picked up, it was followed by a pounding on her front door.

Samantha strode into her room minutes later with her arms crossed and a mixture of concern and consternation twisting her face. She had a bag hanging from one arm and the smell of cinnamon teased Ellie upright. Her cousin's lips twitched. "I swear, if I didn't show up, you'd live as a hermit except for work."

"And grocery shopping."

Samantha snapped her fingers and sat on the edge of the bed. "Really though, Ellie, this isn't normal. You're young and beautiful but you're too tired to enjoy it. Is it worth all this?"

"To have my own business someday, yes." Ellie gave an emphatic nod and infused her voice with the hope she needed to get through each moment of doubt. "When I own my own bakery, I'll set the hours."

"Yes. And you'll be responsible for everything. It'll be up to you to check the work that's going on. Running your own place is a noble quest, but it's tons of work. More work than what you're doing now."

She had a point, but Ellie didn't back down. "This is what I want."

"Okay." Sam pulled the bag from her arm and waved it side to side. "I had to make sure you really meant it, because if you open your own bakery, I'm going to need you to make these."

"Cinnamon rolls?" Ellie almost curled her nose. Not in disgust. She loved cinnamon rolls. They were easy. Almost too easy for her to bother with. There were two other places on Nantucket already making the sweet breakfast roll. She had higher aspirations.

"Oh, come on. Everyone loves cinnamon rolls. They're the perfect breakfast food." Samantha took two rolls from the bag and passed one to Ellie. When Ellie's mouth was full of warm and gooey dough, Samantha pounced. "What's with you and Jarrad?"

Ellie choked and coughed into her fist. What about her and Jarrad. There was nothing to tell. They were . . . friends?

Yes. Friends.

After helping him Wednesday, she'd felt a shift in her feelings for him. Her parents trusted him not only to clean the units but to take on minor repairs without their supervision. That said more than the hitch in her breath when she smelled his cologne or the way her heart jumped when he gave her that certain look.

Thinking of him sent her heart thumping, but she shook her head at Samantha. "There's nothing between me and Jarrad."

"That's not what I asked, but I find your phrasing suspicious. Do you want there to be something between you two?" She bit into her cinnamon roll and wiped a glob of icing from her chin.

Ellie mimicked the action and sank into her fluffy pillows. She picked at the blanket with her clean hand. What did she want? Jarrad was, Jarrad. A month ago, that would have sent her running away. Now it caused her skin to tingle and her cheeks to grow warm. She'd thought he might kiss her Wednesday night and had been disappointed when he didn't. What did that mean?

"I don't know." The honesty of her answer hurt. She wanted her bakery. And she wanted a life of her own outside of work. Were the two mutually exclusive? Could one not exist in the other's presence?

Another knock sounded on her door. Ellie's heart thudded. She squeaked and looked down at her ratty shirt and shorts hidden under the covers.

"I'll get it." Samantha rose in a fluid motion. "You better get up and get dressed. Whoever's out there didn't come for me." She glided away while licking the icing from her fingers. Seconds later, her voice lifted. "Jarrad! What a surprise. What are you doing here?"

"Is Ellie home? I need to talk to her."

"And you couldn't call?"

Ellie listened close to Samantha's tone. It would tell her everything she needed to know. Right now, it said she was intrigued with Jarrad's arrival but not concerned. Her cousin laughed, a full, rich sound that had Ellie diving from the bed and into her closet for a decent shirt and a pair of cute shorts that showed off her legs.

She scrambled into the bathroom to wash her face and brush her teeth. The closed door muffled the voices but didn't drown out Samantha's laughter. What was so funny?

Her hair was a mass of tangles, so she swooped it into a loose bun and dashed from the bathroom, banging her knee on the side table in the hallway. She stumbled into the living room still rubbing her throbbing knee and found Jarrad sitting on the couch with his elbows on his knees. Laughter glittered in his eyes and his smile turned on full wattage as he looked her up and down.

"Hi." Ellie forced the word to sound normal though her pulse pounded, and her breathing was somewhat ragged from her mad dash.

Jarrad stood. "Hey yourself."

"How do you know where I live?" The question barreled out and was followed by a soft moan.

His smile lost its luster. "It's Nantucket. Everyone knows where you live, but if you need specifics, Nathan told me."

It's Nantucket. Boy if those words didn't fit. No one had secrets around here. But Nathan? Tim she could believe. He thrived on chaos and mayhem. It was one of the reasons he stayed on the mainland most of the time. He could wreak more havoc there. She loved her brother, truly, but she didn't always like him. Or what he did to other people.

Especially Lauren. Thank goodness Lauren finally found a guy worthy of her. Seth was exactly what she needed.

"Earth to Ellie." Jarrad moved toward her, his shoulders rising and falling in silent laughter.

"What? I'm contemplating punishment for my brother. He shouldn't give out personal information like that."

"Can you contemplate and ride a bicycle at the same time?" Jarrad ushered her toward the door. "I've something to show you."

She dug her heels into the carpet and soft though it was, she felt the burn across her feet. "Where are we going?"

Jarrad locked eyes with her, willing her to meet his gaze. "You want to see this. Trust me."

Trust him. Did she dare?

Samantha gouged her back. "Oh, go already. It's Nantucket. What's the worst that could happen?" Her laughter broke Ellie's hold on the ground and pushed her forward.

She shoved her feet into a pair of shoes and pocketed her phone and keys. "Lock up for me."

"You bet." Sam answered as the door clicked and Ellie was left on the porch with Jarrad.

The excitement built until she couldn't stand still. "Where are we going?"

"It's a surprise." He straddled a black bicycle and strapped on a helmet. "You're going to love it."

Ellie retrieved her own pink bike from the corner of the porch and joined Jarrad on the paved driveway. She loved riding across Nantucket. The smell of the air soothed while the exercise allowed her to eat her fill of sweets without worrying about fitting into her clothes. But riding with Jarrad was different. A charge filled the air, each stroke of the pedal pushing her questions to the surface.

They rode toward downtown Nantucket. Jarrad pedaled beside her, his breaths short and even.

Hers grew more labored, but she ignored the pinch in her right side and scanned the buildings and people they passed. Cobblestoned streets made her tires bounce but the beauty surrounding Ellie held tight. How often did she simply look at the place she called home? Not often enough. Its beauty took her breath and held it captive.

Their tiny island was glorious to behold.

Jarrad slowed to a stop at the Old Bike Company and removed his helmet. "Here we are."

Ellie looked around, seeing nothing but the shops she saw every day as she traversed this road on her way to the Club Car. "What am I missing? Do you need a new tire for your bike or something?"

"Across the street." Jarrad motioned with his chin but didn't point.

Ellie followed his line of sight. The shallow blue building had been home to many businesses over the years but now sat dark and forlorn amid the hustle and bustle.

Glass windows framed the front of the building, the cedar shingles weathered and warped in the salty air. And there, in the window, a 'for rent' sign that she'd missed. "I didn't know the Fontaines were renting the place."

"Just dropped the notice in the paper this morning." Jarrad's smile was one hundred percent pride. He crossed his arms, still astride his bike though his feet were firmly planted on the ground. "Came to get you soon as I read it. It's perfect. Nice location." He nodded toward the crowds making their way down the street. "You'll be one of a few food businesses in the area, and a great stop for the non-foodies to stop in for breakfast or a dessert to take home as they leave work."

Ellie chewed her lip and rolled the idea around. "Why show it to me? Why not take it for yourself?"

"I'm not ready." He didn't look at her, and she took a moment to memorize his profile before he turned and caught her staring. "You're ready for the next step in the process. What kind of man would I be if I held back, kept the information for myself, then someone else snatches it up?"

He'd be the man she expected based on their past.

He was changing her expectations of him. Every time he showed he'd grown up, it surprised her. Ellie forced herself to let go of the past she held in a stranglehold. Jarrad wasn't the same kid. He wasn't a kid at all. She knew it, but she'd not accepted it.

"Thank you." Stepping away from the bike, she leaned it against the side of a building and threw her arms around Jarrad's neck. "Thank you."

"You're welcome. I said I wanted to help. I meant it." His hands slid around her back and held her close.

Ellie breathed in the sharp tang of his cologne mixed with sweat and sunshine. His chin scraped the crown of her head and she pulled back enough to see his face. *Bad move.* His lips were right there, in her line of sight, and they drew her forward.

Soft. His lips were soft as butter and warm as they touched hers. His fingertips spasmed along her spine before he pulled her closer, crushing her to his chest.

Her world exploded behind closed eyelids. Whirls of color and sensation threw themselves into a kaleidoscope that danced as awareness tapped its way through every point of contact. Her hands wrapped around the back of Jarrad's neck, and the outside world ceased to exist. She could live in this moment forever.

Too soon, Jarrad shifted and broke away.

Ellie's breaths were short and sharp as she struggled to regain her mental footing.

She hadn't meant to kiss him, but now that she had, she'd never forget it. Never stop thinking about it. About him.

JARRAD LET THE SENSATION of kissing Ellie slide through him, filling him with enough joy to last a lifetime. He longed to kiss her again. Maybe even forever, but not here in the middle of town. They'd drawn a bit of attention already. A group of women giggled from across the street. While he wasn't shy, kissing Ellie's socks off didn't need an audience.

"Do you want to see inside?" He kicked himself for drawing her attention back to the building, but it was either that or keep staring at her like he'd never seen a woman before.

She ran her hands over her head and patted the knot of hair on the back of her neck. He'd dislodged a bit of it but not enough to be troublesome apparently since she didn't bother fixing it. A delicate shrug and she lifted her eyes to his. Deep, deep blue.

His throat grew too dry to swallow. To speak required too much effort. Ellie had no idea how gorgeous she was. Even this just-rolled-out-of-bed look suited her.

"Can we?" Her voice cracked. She blushed and took a step back, making him realize he'd not moved his arms from around her.

His fingers trailed around her ribs before falling free and thumping to his thighs. Why did they feel like they no longer belonged to him?

"I called the Fontaines and they left a key for us." He swung his leg over the bicycle seat and kicked the stand down to keep the bike from toppling over. He grabbed Ellie's hand, loving the feel of her soft palm against his. He squeezed and pulled her to his side before darting across the empty street.

Not many cars to worry about, even here in the middle of town. Most people walked or rode bikes. It was part of why he loved the little island.

He retrieved the key from behind a loose brick propped beside the door. The key stuck halfway into the lock. Jarrad wiggled the knob, then the key. Sweat trickled down the side of his face.

Ellie leaned her back on the building and crossed her arms. "I'm thinking you didn't call the Fontaines." She grinned and tapped her toes. "I'm thinking you found that key, assumed it went to this door, and now you're trying to impress me."

"If I wanted to impress you, I'd have taken you on a helicopter ride around the island." He grunted when the key slipped and jabbed his palm. "If I did find this random key under a brick, I'd have tried it first before going all the way to your house and back again."

He shimmed the key side to side. With a crack, it sheared off. The force behind his maneuvering sent his knuckles skipping over the knob. Skin split and peeled back as it caught on the fragment of exposed key. "Whoops." He grimaced at the burn and shook his hand.

"I take it back." Ellie reached for his hand and clicked her tongue. "We should get that cleaned up."

"It's nothing." He pulled his hand away from her touch before he lost all sense and kissed her again.

Ellie cupped her hands around her eyes and peered through the windows. "Looks good in there."

"Let me check something." He jogged to the back of the building. A rickety door hung at an angle, the hinges nearly rusted through. Not good, but good for what he had in mind. He wouldn't have to bust the door down. One heavy shove with his shoulder and the weathered frame turned into kindling. He fell through the opening with a cough and a wheeze. Musty air filled his lungs.

Ellie gaped at him from the front window. She rapped on the glass. "You're going to get us arrested. That's breaking and entering."

Jarrad waved a hand at her as a surge of adrenaline peaked in his bloodstream. A twist of the lock and the front door opened. He waved Ellie inside. "They said we were allowed to check out the building. Not my fault I checked out the back door and found rotting wood, which will be great at driving down the price."

Ellie's pert nose wrinkled. "That doesn't seem fair."

"They didn't keep up proper maintenance on the building, Ellie. That isn't your fault. I'm a pushover but even I won't let them try and get top dollar out of a renter when their back door was literally hanging by a thread."

Her snort echoed in the emptiness. "Says the man who burst in like a linebacker."

"Oh no. We're not switching to sports. We associate based on movies and pop culture. I've never been interested in football." He spun an empty rack where postcards once rested. The metal screeched and whined before the entire contraption toppled over. Okay then. He looked over at Ellie, whose wide eyes took in his every move. "We'll call this a recon mission. Like—"

"Like Bruce Willis in *Fifth Element*."

Impressive. He could get used to being Bruce Willis. "I'll be Bruce as long as I get to keep my hair." He ran a hand over his head. He'd worked hard to find the perfect cut. It wasn't easy maintaining a style like his.

"As long as you don't think I'm going to dye mine orange and run around in a jumpsuit that looks like it went three rounds with a lawnmower." Her entire body shook as laughter rang out.

He loved that sound. She kept it bottled up too often. The world needed Ellie Jones' laughter. He needed it. Every day. "Deal." He stuck out his hand and she shook it once.

The old building was perfect for Ellie. A low counter cut across half the space. Shelves went from the floor to the ceiling along one wall. A perfect place for displays of cookies and other goodies. He moved into the kitchen, which was compact but had potential.

Ellie joined him. She pursed her lips and whistled. "Needs a few changes in here to be functional."

"Another reason you'll get a great price. None of this is up to code, especially not for a kitchen."

"Well, it's never been used for the kitchen before. Candle shop. Boutique. I forget what it was before that." Ellie continued to stroll around the space. She trailed a hand over the pale blue walls. "I like the color, but not what I had in mind."

"Don't tell me." He put his fingers to his temples and closed his eyes, doing his best "Psych" impression. "You wanted pink walls. Yellow trim. And alternating colors of purple and green on the shelves."

Her laughter turned the room bright with joy. "And with that, I will say you are fired as an interior decorator. I do not want my shop looking like a unicorn threw up inside."

"And here I thought I knew you." He threw his hands up in the air, then winked to make sure she knew he was joking. "What do you think? Are you sold?"

"I need to crunch the numbers. Once I know what they are." But her head was bobbing up and down.

He could see the excitement in every motion. She continued touching everything within sight.

"Not a bad ride into town. About the same as riding to the restaurant." She frowned then. "I'll have to tell Connor I'm leaving. If I'm leaving. You'll help me with the contract?" The hope in her voice undid him and made him want to offer her the world in a snow globe so she could have everything in the palm of her hand.

"I'll call Monday and make an appointment." He locked the front door back and helped Ellie step over the debris from his fight with the back door. After putting the door back, as close to closing as it would go, he propped several boards in front of the cracks to hide them from view. "I'll come back later and fix it." Ellie made to move away. Jarrad stopped her, taking her hand and lacing their fingers together. "You want to go somewhere with me?"

A single nod.

How did the tiniest of motions make his entire body shift? Ellie wanted to spend time with him. Him. The kid who pranked her to the point she hated his guts. Now she willingly let her hand rest in his and smiled. He might find his way and build a life of his own after all.

Chapter Eight

THEY RODE EAST UNTIL they reached the Coskata-Coatue Wildlife Reserve. Ellie wheeled into the scrap of a parking lot and stopped for a breather. Seven and a half miles. They'd ridden halfway across Nantucket. Winded didn't begin to describe the searing in her lungs. "Where are we going?" She wheezed with each word.

Jarrad nodded at the gatehouse. A tiny, shingled building with red trim hardly big enough for a single person to stand inside. "You're still asking that question." He laughed, full and rich.

"Can't help it. I have a need-to-know personality."

"Which is why taking you by surprise is so much fun."

That explained a few things. Like his constant drive to push her outside her comfort zone. She lived within the known. He thrived on the unknown.

He walked his bike toward a post and locked it in place. "No more bikes. Until we head home, anyway." The delight in his smile caused her own lips to try and match his. A set of keys jingled in his hand. "Now for the fun part."

Ellie looked around for a car, but the lot was empty except for a small four-wheeler. Sunlight glinted off the green plastic. "You expect me to ride that? With you." A chance to wrap her arms around his waist and press close. Her fingers curled into her palms. She wouldn't be surprised to have a flashing warning sign suddenly appear. Dangerous territory. And she wanted to step over the threshold more than she'd wanted anything in a long time.

She could have both a new bakery and a love life. People did it every day.

Jarrad didn't answer, just stood there swinging the keys back and forth. Unhurried. Like he had all day to wait on her.

Ellie swallowed her doubts and took a step toward the quad. "I'll make a deal with you."

"I'm listening."

"We take turns driving."

The keys stopped moving. Seagulls swooped overhead—their calls shrill in the morning air. One dove and landed a foot away from Jarrad. He eyed the bird, then faced her. "You know how to drive a quad in the sand?"

"Oh, come on. I've lived here my entire life. Of course, I know how to drive on the sand. I should be asking you that." She grinned to take any sting from her words. This adventure was about having fun, and she wanted her own slice of it. Which included being in the driver's seat. If Jarrad could stomach turning over control. A better test had never been created than to ask for the keys to what most considered a man's toy.

"Okay. I drive there. You drive back." He winked and tilted his head. "Figured out where we're going?"

"The lighthouse." It made perfect sense now that she'd seen the machine. After a seven-mile bike ride, the last thing she wanted was to walk another seven miles in the sand to reach the beacon of hope on Nantucket's northern-most point. It was the brightest lighthouse in New England. A fact they took pride in despite the lighthouse not being allowed on the National Register of Historic Places thanks to being rebuilt twice. No way she'd dare pass up a chance to ride a quad down that same stretch of beach.

Jarrad slid onto the padded seat and waited for her to join him. "I let air out of the tires already so it'll be easier to drive, but you should hold on to me anyway." The twinkle in his eyes said more than the smile.

Ellie was happy to comply. She swung her leg over and settled on the edge of the seat. One good jostle and her tailbone would hit the metal railing behind her. The companies really should consider making a longer seat. Then again, if she had more space, she'd be less likely to lean so close to Jarrad's back.

She looped her arms around his waist and tucked her cheek into the center of his spine. The engine growled to life and rumbled beneath her. Jarrad's back was warm on her skin. She waited for movement, but they sat quietly, breathing together for several heartbeats before he ran a rough palm over her arm and squeezed. Her heart hiccupped.

He popped the gears with his foot and thumbed the gas, sending them rolling across the sand and down a narrow path. Tall dunes covered in grasses flashed by. She couldn't see over Jarrad's shoulder to watch the path, so she contented herself with the view from the side. It was worth a bit of sweat and the heat radiating from his back to feel solid muscle beneath her palms.

Ellie tightened her grip to stop her hands from roaming. They wanted a mind of their own and the freedom to explore. Not happening. The miles passed too fast as sand sprayed behind the tires. They passed seagulls and cranes but no people. Ellie rubbed a strand of hair away from her nose and grinned. They might have the entire lighthouse to themselves.

"It's about to get rough." Jarrad turned his head enough to shout over his shoulder but kept both hands on the handlebars.

She took that as a sign to hold on tighter and squeezed herself to his back. Wind whistled around them. Jarrad blocked most of the breeze, but a bit teased the hair falling from her bun and sent it flying into her face. One strand lifted and draped itself around Jarrad's neck. He shivered under her hands.

Did this ride affect him? The ride back with her in the front suddenly seemed like a foolish idea. How would she concentrate? It didn't seem possible. He'd taken everything she knew about him and turned it upside down. His work ethics and drive were near hers, on a level she never expected. Which reminded her. How did he manage to have a Saturday off? The same Saturday as her? Something fishy with that.

The quad rolled to a stop.

Ellie popped her head up from Jarrad's back. His t-shirt stuck to her face and forced her to peel the material away. She looked left and right and found nothing but grass, an entire field of it. "Why'd we stop? The lighthouse is up ahead."

"I wanted us to see it together." He shifted and faced her. "You can't see from back there, and it's too pretty to miss. Let's walk the rest of the way."

Ellie hopped off the machine and straightened her clothes, then attempted to tuck her hair back into the bun.

Jarrad stopped her with a hand on her shoulder. "Leave it. You look good with your hair all wild and carefree."

Which meant she looked like the wicked witch in the *Wizard of Oz*. But she'd let it go. The chances of taming it without a mirror and a brush were zero so what did it matter.

Jarrad took her hand, once again winding their fingers together. A single move that no doubt millions of people did every day, yet it felt intimate in this moment with him. She'd never really thought about it before, how touching someone caused a chain reaction through her body. Likely because she'd never experienced it until Jarrad. He forced her out of the little box she'd drawn for herself and showed her the vividness of life in all its bold glory.

Moving as one, they walked the sandy path, winding their way around a bend and bringing the lighthouse into full view. White against a backdrop of blue, it split the sky in a vertical slash and drew her eyes up and up to that flashing beacon that offered both hope and warning to those at sea.

How many sailors were drawn to its glow in the midst of turbulent waters and felt hope spring up with every flash?

She felt it now, with Jarrad's hand against hers and their strides moving in tandem. This is what life was meant to be like for her. It didn't have to be serious all the time. Jarrad balanced her need for order, and she liked to think she tempered his insatiable desire to prank those around him.

WHEN HE FIRST ASKED Ellie to join him, Jarrad had expected her to say no. He'd planned this for days but barricaded his heart against the possibility of a yes. The lighthouse was spectacular, but nothing compared to the look on Ellie's face. He kicked through the sand until they were within touching distance of the stark white walls.

Ellie reached out and braced her palm on the lighthouse. Jarrad followed, surprised to find the stone cold despite the heat bearing down on them. He'd felt his skin frying as they biked over and thanked his lucky stars there was a constant breeze coming up from the ocean to keep him from being completely disgusting when Ellie put her arms around him.

If only he'd packed a picnic. Or any kind of food. Note to self: prepare better next time. If there was a next time.

Jarrad scanned the beach. Not a soul in sight.

"Are you excited about the building?" He grimaced at the mundane conversation starter, but he couldn't jump right in and say, *Hey, I think I really like you. Want to date?* Well. He could. And then he could watch as Ellie ran screaming the other way. Best to ease into the situation. Test the waters. He was Egon. Thoughtful and loyal.

Ellie's sigh met the wind and raced away. "I can't believe you found a place that fast. I've been planning and dreaming for so long. Now it's right here and it doesn't seem real. I keep expecting to wake up."

"This is no dream. Trust me. If it was, there would be food. And I wouldn't have to go to work this afternoon."

"Ah." Ellie nodded. "I wondered how you had a day off." She squinted at him and tented one hand over her eyes, never letting go of his hand with the other. "Why are you on afternoons? I needed you in the mornings."

"Connor pulled me off mornings. Said he needed me in the afternoon." So much more he wanted to say. About how Connor wanted Ellie to himself and was doing this to keep Jarrad away from her. But that was all speculation and served no purpose other than to make himself feel better by spilling the words binding themselves around his heart. That he wasn't enough for Ellie. His aspirations of head chef or possible business owner were fledglings without feathers. They were untested against Ellie's folders and stacks of papers outlining every advantage and disadvantage. He'd seen them piled three inches high on her coffee table this morning.

Ellie only shook her head and moved around the lighthouse, taking him with her unless he released her hand. "What's your favorite breakfast food?"

"You're asking me about food when I'm starving to death? That's just mean." He lowered his eyebrows in mock annoyance, but his smile kept his true feelings on display. "Those cinnamon rolls you had this morning smelled delicious. Wouldn't mind having one of those right now." He rubbed his stomach, and a low rumble gripped the muscles.

Ellie rolled her eyes. "Everyone wants cinnamon rolls. Okay. What about after dinner? Exotic flavors? What about a dragon fruit tart?"

"Uh, no thanks. Peach turnovers?"

"Too easy." She paced toward the water.

Jarrad kicked off his shoes and sank his bare feet into the sand. White granules pressed between his toes and the heat seeped deep into his bones. "So you're going for sophisticated." He rubbed his thumb over her knuckles. "You gotta do Cannoli's then. I didn't get to try the Choux pastry, but that's another option. What about a pie of the day, but spice it up? Or do fried fruit pies. Simple but classic and people can eat them on the go. People love foods they can eat while they walk around and shop. Or donuts." The rumble in his belly grew to a roar.

Ellie threw her head back and laughed. "Okay. I get the point. You're hungry."

"Let's get something to eat."

She made a point of looking around. "Sure. Let's pop into that imaginary bakery behind the lighthouse and have a slice of pie."

"You kid, but that would be a nice place for a restaurant." He motioned at the empty coastline. "Except, you know, for the lack of foot traffic. But boy it'd be nice right about now."

Because they had nearly eight miles of bike riding ahead of them. And that was if he survived the drive back with Ellie at the wheel. He trusted her driving abilities. He didn't trust himself to have free access to hold her during the driving. Having her arms around him had sent a super charge of attraction racing though his blood and he'd barely managed to keep it contained.

Having the shoe on the other foot, so to speak, was not something he looked forward to as much as he ached for the contact. He'd done it. Just like that, he'd gone and fallen head over heels for her.

It wasn't love, this emotion deep down inside. Infatuation. Curiosity. Delight. But not love. Not yet.

"You want to go out sometime?"

Ellie's quick grin sent a race of heat through him. "I thought that's what we were doing right now."

"Dinner. Would you like to go to dinner with me? With real food and everything." Say yes. Please, say yes. He wanted to learn more about her. Her hopes and dreams. Her fears. He knew plenty, but not enough. He needed to know everything.

"As long as we don't go to the Club Car, it's a date." Her eyebrows shot toward her hairline. "You meant it to be a date, right? Because if you didn't, I didn't mean to imply. You just—"

"It's a date. I would love to go on a date with you. I'll even bring you flowers and wear clothes that don't have holes in them." He ran his finger through the twin holes at the bottom of his shirt and wiggled it side to side. "We'll go somewhere nice. Like Slip 14."

"Dinner with a view. I like it." Ellie took a deep breath, and her face took on a look he knew too well. It said she wanted to say something, and he probably wouldn't like it. Jarrad braced for impact as she spoke again. "You're not who I thought you were."

"Um. Thanks? I wanted to be Steven Seagal, but I don't have the face for that mustache."

Ellie whacked his arm with the back of her hand. "I'm serious. When you showed up, I was on edge, waiting for you to sneak into my house and hide a snake in my bed. Stuff like you did when we were kids."

"I won't say I never considered it, but I want to think I've changed since then."

"You have. I thought you were a spoiled, rich kid who'd come back to Nantucket to goof off while his parents paid his bills."

Ouch. "Tell me how you really feel. Don't hold back."

She had the decency to wince. "Sorry. I'm glad I was wrong. You work hard at the restaurant and at the resort. I've never seen you shirk a duty, and you're always willing to go above and beyond what anyone asks of you." She squeezed his hand and stopped walking while turning to face him. Her chin tipped up. "I misjudged you, and I'm sorry about that. I've never been happier to be so incredibly wrong. Especially about you."

Well if that didn't ice the cake and toss on a pile of ice cream. He'd managed to impress her without even trying.

"My parents are rich, but they've never paid my bills. Dad doesn't believe in handouts, which is why I'm here making my own way instead of doing things his way. I don't like real estate. I don't like deceiving people. And I do like to prank people from time to time. Laughter is the best medicine, right?"

He wouldn't say sharing was caring. Sharing his darkest pieces with Ellie hurt. The look of sympathy in her eyes and the way the bands around his chest loosened made it worthwhile. He could learn to share more if it meant it brought them closer.

Chapter Nine

THE MEETING WITH THE Fontaines went better than Ellie dreamed possible. Mostly because of Jarrad. He'd negotiated with the couple like it was his own business on the line. He'd pointed out all the places in the old building where updates were necessary, and lack of care had caused problems with the walls and floor. But he never lost his temper or became condescending like his dad often did when his parents visited Nantucket. She liked the Olsons, but they were a bit snobby if she let herself be honest.

Admitting it even to herself sent a prickle of unease along her spine. She was going on a date with Jarrad and putting his parents down, albeit mentally. She had no right. Stiffening her spine, Ellie walked into the kitchen at the Club Car and waved for Connor. From this point on, she would do her best to view his parents through the same perspective she saw Jarrad. She'd put them in a box and labeled it without knowing anything about the people she was judging. Her parents raised her better than that, and she determined to prove herself worthy of the respect.

Better yet, to extend that respect to everyone she met.

Connor tossed a towel over his left shoulder and propped his hands on his hips. "What's up?"

"Can we talk somewhere private?" She tilted her head toward every listening ear.

A grin broke through his sternness. "Sure." He motioned her toward the pantry and closed the door behind them.

"I want to open my own bakery."

"That's great." Genuine enthusiasm shone from his eyes.

"In two months."

The light blinked out from his expression. "Oh." He fingered the towel. "That's awful fast, isn't it?"

"I have a building. It'll take some work. Long days, but I'm used to that already." She patted his arm and paused to squeeze his hand. "I'll keep working here until the weekend before opening. I wanted to let you know first so you could look for a replacement." Here was the hardest part. Ellie swallowed to ease the tightness in her throat. "I'd like to offer my bakery as your preferred option for buying bread and pastries. I'll give you a premium price and guarantee the product."

"Two months." Connor's blink was long and slow. He breathed deeply and let it out in a rush. "You need employees. Clients. A marketing strategy. It's a lot to do. Are you sure you're ready?" He shook his head before she could answer. "Forget I said that. You wouldn't jump into something this big without being prepared. We're too much alike in that regard."

He had that right. It was why they worked so well together and how she knew she could trust him with the information.

"I'd be honored to be a client of yours, Ellie. I'll clear it with the owners. They love your bread so I'm sure it won't be a problem." He cocked his head and started to run a hand through his hair. He caught the net and grimaced.

Ellie rose to her toes and clapped. "Oh, thank you. You won't regret it. I'll have the bread and pastries delivered fresh every morning. It's going to be great."

"Yep. Great." His voice was muffled and soft, making her listen hard for the words. He lifted his head and smiled. "I should get back to work. You here for a few hours?"

"Sure." She'd come in early to bake then ran out for the meeting. It only made sense that she would stick around now and finish everything for tomorrow. Ellie twirled in a circle as Connor left the pantry. She had a building and her first client. Next stop, employees. And a menu.

Oh, and to stop by the building with Jarrad to make a list of all the repairs and changes she wanted to make.

The next months were bound to be insane with plans, but it would all be worth it to see her name hanging from a cute sign over the door. Or maybe in the window. She needed a logo. The possibilities swirled in bright streams of color. Each idea shot off into a bold line. Ellie reeled them in one by one. First, finish her shift.

She raced through the next morning's prep, the hours flying by in a flurry of dough, yeast, and milk. Thoughts of Jarrad joined her as she read the recipe and grabbed the yeast from the shelf. They'd gone from her high animosity and concern over pranks to trusting him to help get her building up to code.

Finally, the last batch of bread was ready to set aside for the morning. Ellie washed the bits of flour from her fingers and waved goodbye. Becky shouted an enthusiastic goodbye while Connor frowned. Ellie let it all slide from her shoulders and jogged down the streets, hooking lefts and rights until she reached her blue building. The color had to go, but it wasn't a priority.

Jarrad waited for her, standing with his back against the building and his arms crossed. He should be on a postcard. The image was perfectly casual and hip with Nantucket sweeping across the backdrop and the warm blue tones accentuating his dark hair.

"Hey." She sounded out of breath but put it off on the jog and not on how pretty Jarrad looked. Yes. Pretty. He had handsome down pat, but men could be pretty too.

He smirked at her—a look she was coming to realize meant he was happy to see her. "Ready for the hard part?" He produced a key and shook it.

"You mean getting in through the front door? Got a trick to that besides busting down the back door again?"

"Hardy har-har. You're hilarious." He held out the key. "Give it a try."

She looked from him to the shiny knob near his elbow. A new brass knob greeted her. She grasped it in her palm and relished the warm metal before sliding the key in and turning it to the right. A quick *snick* sent her nerves shooting to the surface. Would the place look different now that she'd signed the papers and made it official? Buyer's remorse was a real thing. She'd felt it before after spending a hundred bucks on a beautiful top, the one she'd worn to the clambake and then regretted it the next morning.

No. She would not let herself regret this. Telling her parents might change her mind. When would be a good time to tell them she was quitting the resort? There was no such thing as a perfect time, but she couldn't drag it out. They needed to find someone else to handle the books.

Tomorrow. She'd tell them tomorrow. Her lungs filled with a breath, and she stepped inside with Jarrad a step behind. "We have to get rid of that smell." Her nose curled at the musty aroma. It hadn't dissipated despite opening both doors this morning while they spoke with the Fontaines.

"I can fix that." Jarrad pulled his phone from his pocket and tapped.

"What are you doing?"

"Making a list. Remove odor. Check." He swiped and grinned. "Couple air fresheners and you're all set."

"Jarrad. Be serious."

"Ellie. Take a breath. If you get too wrapped up in every tiny detail, you'll drive yourself crazy. I was joking about the air fresheners. Bake a loaf of bread and it'll never know what hit it."

A snort of laughter escaped. "You're not wrong."

"I know. I'm also craving bread. You didn't happen to bring any leftovers, did you?" He gave her a puppy dog look and poked out his bottom lip.

"Pick that thing up before you trip over it." She ran her fingers over the counter, delighted with the smooth texture. "What do you think is under this?"

"Wood."

"What kind?"

"No idea. It was probably gorgeous once upon a time. Who knows what it would look like now?" He rocked his head and studied the rows of shelves. "We could sand it all off and see. Have to sand all the old paint away before we can cover it anyway. Might find a goldmine of original wood under there."

"Put that on the list. If we start sanding and it doesn't look good, we'll paint."

"Got it." He tapped and swiped.

They were doing this. They were acting like a team. "Are you a contractor?"

"No. But I'm your contractor."

"What does that mean?" She didn't mean to ask so many questions, but every answer he gave only stimulated the need to know more. Why was he helping?

THIS WAS IT. HIS CHANCE to ask the question that had been burning through him since Ellie mentioned her shop. They could work together every day. The words lodged in his chest, held fast to his heart. Working together could drive them apart. But what if it didn't? He shoved the possible consequences aside. This was the type of move he lived for. To jump in and start treading water. "I have the contacts you need to get this place ready. I want to help. And once it's running, I want to work for you."

Ellie stilled. Frozen. Her mouth dropped open. Ellie, speechless? It had to be a record.

Seconds passed, each one accounted for in his thudding heartbeat. Why did it take her so long to answer?

"You'd have to work the morning shift." The words seemed to pull up from her toes they took so long to appear. Even when they were said, she remained motionless. Poised as a bird in fear for its life.

Mornings. He could do it.

"You couldn't work afternoons for Connor and be here for the daylight shift. I don't mean mornings as in ten. I mean four. Before daylight. And you would work until noon." She wrung her hands.

He didn't know people actually did that, but Ellie did. Her fingers twisted and turned until her knuckles turned red. The look on her face was unusual. He didn't understand it. A mixture between concern and denial. What was she worried about?

"I'll do it." He opened a new list on his phone and typed: Quit the restaurant. He couldn't wait to see the look on Connor's face. Jarrad's skills were wasted there anyway. He had a culinary degree and all he was trusted with was fried eggs. "I can have a carpenter here as early as tomorrow if you're ready to get started."

"Am I?" Ellie shoved her hands into her pockets and turned. Her gaze skipped around the room. "I want an industrial sink in the kitchen. And two ovens. Maybe three. Depends on the baking load. Should I aim high or be realistic?"

This was why they worked. "Dream big. Go for three." He continued the list. "We need an electrician to check the wiring. I have last year's inspection, and it checked out, but I want it redone before we start messing around with additional stoves. If the inspection fails, then we find a new building. I made that part of your contract. You're not responsible for repairing or overcoming anything that was overlooked by previous tenants."

He'd done his best by Ellie. The last thing he wanted was for her to fail. She'd never dare to risk another dream if this one flopped. He'd make sure it didn't. They would be one of those teams who held each other up. Like the carpenter crews he watched on TV, the husband and wife team. He always forgot their names.

Muted light gleamed in her eyes, and they shone back at him with the light of anticipation.

"You've thought of everything."

Not everything, but enough to get her started.

There was a softness to her as she stood there, and a need to stay close filled him. She could do this on her own, but he wanted to be there and see her succeed.

"What will you do about the resort? I don't see you working with me and cleaning at night either. It's too much. I stop by to do the books and I'm exhausted. I can't imagine something as tiring as cleaning."

She did often remind him of a perpetually exhausted seagull. Ellie swooped in, got the job done, and disappeared until the next time she was needed.

"I'll figure something out. Of course, you could pay me an exorbitant amount of money, then I wouldn't have to worry about paying rent." He laughed and strode deeper into the kitchen where an old refrigerator chugged away, zapping the electricity. "Why is this on?" He pulled the door handle. Nothing. The door fought back, refusing to budge. "We'll see about that."

"Maybe you should leave it alone." Ellie suggested from the doorway. She wrinkled her nose in a snarl. "Maybe that's where the smell is coming from."

Jarrad planted his foot on the counter beside the door, grasped the handle with both hands, and heaved. His grunt was overthrown by the groan of the door. "There. See, it's—"

Crash.

The door broke loose from the hinges and fell to the floor, taking Jarrad with it. He went down hard. His foot slid from the counter and threatened to jerk him into the splits.

Ellie's scream cut off as she gagged. "I'm out of here. That one is all yours."

A stomach-wrenching stench filled the air. It was so thick it spilled down his throat and coated his nose until all he smelled was the rottenness that billowed from the moldy interior. Not a single item was distinguishable as food. Everywhere he looked was covered in mold and filth. The stench caused his stomach to roll. Breathing through his mouth made it worse.

He gagged and pushed to his feet. Maybe he could get the door back on and seal the smell back inside.

Nope.

The door was done, the hinges rusted through. His force and determination sheared them down the middle. Jarrad wiped his hands on his thighs, feeling dirty though he'd not touched anything. He dialed the first number on his contacts list. "Hey, Arnie, got a job for you." He ran from the building. Tears streamed from his eyes.

Ellie fumbled with the door, slamming and locking it behind him.

Great gulps of clean air eased some of the burn from his throat, but he'd never rid his nose of the awful gut-crawling stench. He gave Arnie the details and collapsed on the ground.

"Told you not to open it." Ellie wiped her face and rocked on her heels while peering through the windows. "I swear, I see a billowing cloud of green spilling across the ground like fog."

"Don't touch it. Probably burn you." It certainly burned his eyes. And his nose. Throat. Never again. "I'll never open another door again."

"Then you'll starve to death."

"Nope. Pantry food. Spaghetti. Soup. Heat it and eat it." He cleared another wave of tears attempting to wash the smell from his eyes. It didn't make sense, but a smell that strong affected every sense.

"Where's Slimer when you need him?" Ellie lowered herself to the ground beside him. She took a short breath and pushed back to her feet. "You need a shower. And you'd better burn those clothes."

Great. These were his favorite shorts.

"Hey, Ellie?" He waited for her to look down at him. "Who you gonna call?"

"Not the Ghostbusters." She tapped the glass. "Not an exterminator. Maybe a hazmat team." Holding out a hand, she motioned for him. "Come on. Maybe we'll get lucky, and the smell won't spread beyond our building before your guy gets here. I bet the whole place is going to reek for weeks though. Do we still want the building?"

"Yes. Arnie will take care of everything. I had him on a house once. Last year. Owners were nice, but they had no idea cleaning was even a thing. I kept letting the inspection slide, thought they were doing the best they could. Didn't know how bad things were until it was too late. If you've ever seen *Hoarders,* you know what I mean when I say there was trash to the ceiling in some of the rooms. Arnie had it cleaned up in a couple days. This'll be no problem." Jarrad took her hand and stood. His right thigh seized. Must have pulled something with the he-man heave on the door. No more than he deserved.

They strolled down the street, hand in hand. Ellie looked up at him and brushed a hand over his forehead. The touch blazed through him, and he pulled her to a stop.

"I'm trusting you with this."

Five little words never scared him until now. How was he supposed to respond? Thanks? Here's my heart, I'm trusting you with it, seemed a bit over the top. Unless they were in a high-octane live-or-die situation where Bruce Willis jumped out from around the corner and ushered them into a spaceship . . . Jarrad stopped before he lost his ever-loving mind and looked for the action hero. This was real. A moment where Ellie risked letting him see a part of herself that few ever had.

"I can fix that." The line from *Holes* sprinted from his lips. He groaned and pinched his eyes closed. "That's not what I meant. I won't let you down. That's what I wanted to say."

"If I show up tomorrow with a gun slung around my hips and wearing bright red lipstick, you better run the other way." Ellie put a hand on his chest. She patted him while her lips moved into a smile that sent his heart tripping sideways.

A woman after his own heart.

Chapter Ten

JARRAD STEELED HIS spine and faced Connor. This conversation needed to happen. Nothing to it. "I'd like to switch shifts. Take on the lunch crowd instead of the nights."

Connor's frown pulled his face into a grimace. "Any particular reason?"

"Looking at my options. Making some changes in my life and I need my afternoons free." So he could sleep and wake up early enough to work for Ellie. But Connor didn't need to know that. He forced his muscles to relax and his expression into something like boredom.

"I need time to find someone to cover your shift."

"That's fine. I don't need to change right away." Jarrad clamped his lips closed to keep from giving away too much.

The kitchen bustled with activity. Becky watched the conversation from her station by the doors leading out into the restaurant where Jarrad was supposed to work tonight. He wouldn't miss the late nights and the crowds. He loved working with people, but the time spent with Ellie was worth the early mornings and fatigue he felt pulling at his muscles. They'd hardly begun working out details for her building.

Arnie was there now cleaning up the mess from the refrigerator. Seriously, who left food to rot like that? The Fontaines had claimed they had no idea it was there. Whoever rented the building before must have left it behind. He gave his head a mental shake. This was no time to focus on Ellie.

Connor was eying him with too much knowledge in his gaze. "When's the deadline?"

"What do you mean?"

"When do you need to change shifts? Do I have a month? Two? A week?"

Yep. Definitely suspicious.

Jarrad lifted a hand to his hair and stopped short of running his hands through the mess when Connor made a pointed look at the food around them. Without a hair net, he shouldn't even be this deep in the kitchen right now. It couldn't be helped. As soon as he'd come in for his shift, he'd found himself unable to get started without clearing the air first. Should he tell Connor the truth? "Two months."

The nod said plenty, but Connor crossed his arms and pushed out his chin. "You're going to work with Ellie."

It wasn't a question, so Jarrad didn't answer. "Can you do it?"

"I'll try." The words were right, but Connor's tone said he wouldn't try very hard to accommodate his rival. That's what they'd become the night they both offered to walk Ellie home.

Connor spent more time in the kitchen than any of his workers. He had the dedication part down pat. He'd be a solid match for a woman like Ellie. If Jarrad's heart hadn't already decided he wanted a relationship with Ellie. Backing down was out of the question. He'd invested too much of himself in proving to Ellie that he was worth the risk. They had a chance for this to work.

If he had to spend all his time at the bakery to see her, then so be it. She was worth it.

Jarrad nodded and reached for the apron he wore out of the kitchen to deliver food. "Thanks."

The rest of the night passed without any trouble until he approached a familiar couple sitting at the table in the corner. An inward groan tightened his chest. Forcing a smile, he slid a plate of steak and potatoes in front of the man. "Mr. Townsend, how good to see you again." To the woman, Jarrad offered a Caesar salad with a side of grilled chicken. "Mrs. Townsend, how's your mother?" All he'd heard last time they visited was her mother's long list of ailments. Spread among the complaints over the food.

Mr. Townsend cut into his steak and frowned. "I asked for medium well. This is rare." He shoved a bite into his mouth and chewed while frowning. The man had an excellent frown. A cross between grumpy cat and the Grinch.

Jarrad didn't bother arguing. He knew this couple and where this would lead. The steak was a perfect medium well, as anyone in the kitchen could attest. "Let me take that back to the kitchen for you." He lifted a brow at the woman. "And yours?"

She sniffed the chicken. "This chicken is old." Like her husband, she gorged on a bite before he took the plate away.

Carrying both plates to the kitchen, Jarrad pushed through the doors and held the plates aloft. "Triple threat."

The kitchen fell silence save for the clinking of spoons on pans and the sizzle of meat in skillets.

Connor heaved a breath. "Who?"

"Townsends."

Every staff member groaned.

He took the plates from Jarrad and slid them onto a sliver of empty counter space. "Let me guess. Undercooked."

"Yep. Next it'll be overcooked. After that, probably ask for the manager because no one here knows how to properly cook meat." Jarrad listed the Townsend's typical responses, ticking them off on his fingers.

"Let's head them off right now." Connor reached for two new plates and carried them out. The look on his face had the wait staff scattering.

Jarrad didn't blame them. He'd caught a glimpse of Connor's expression before he left the kitchen. It was borderline maniacal, his eyes glossy and stretched wide. But it was his smile that sent a shudder down Jarrad's spine.

"I'm sorry for your previous meals." Connor dropped the plates onto the table with a thud. "I'm the head chef here at the Club Car, and I personally supervised these dishes. If you find fault with them, I encourage you to come to the kitchen and cook your own." His lip curled. "I've taken the liberty of letting the manager know you're here. I'm sure he'll be more than happy to check on you."

Mr. Townsend cut into his steak and opened his mouth.

Connor lifted an eyebrow. "Medium well, yes? Thin line of pink through the center, seconds from well-done and tender as they come." He said it like a dare, and Mr. Townsend's mouth snapped shut around the bite of steak.

The man chewed and swallowed.

Mrs. Townsend pushed the chicken around on her plate. She cut into a piece and sniffed it delicately. "Was this chicken frozen? It smells frozen."

"No, ma'am, we buy our chicken fresh from the butcher every morning. I can show you, if you like." He pulled his phone from his pocket. "I have pictures of the butchering, plucking, and delivery right here."

She blanched and shuddered. "I believe you."

Connor clapped his hands. "Well then, I think we're all finished here. Please, enjoy your meal. We look forward to serving you again." He spun on his heel, nearly clipping Jarrad's shoulder in the tight quarters.

All around them, diners stared. Connor had kept his voice low, but after enduring this same attitude from the couple for going on a year, Jarrad was thrilled to see it end. A few of the locals grinned and didn't bother hiding their glee.

One man cheered. "Bout time." He winked at Mrs. Townsend. "Sorry, ma'am, but you two had that coming. Good folks here. Great food. Bad attitudes like yours ruins it for everyone. Consider that next time you try and get a free meal with your meanness."

"Well. I never." Mrs. Townsend looked at her husband and scowled. "Aren't you going to do anything about this?"

He shook his head. "Eat your food." He shoveled the steak in like a man starving.

Jarrad retreated to the kitchen where laughter ripped from his chest and joined that of the entire kitchen.

Connor's face was flushed, and he wiped it with a towel. "I shouldn't have done that."

"Are you kidding?" A kid in the back gave a wicked smile. "That was epic."

Jarrad agreed with the rest of the employees still grinning and clapping Connor on the back. He might not have handled it the best, but if it was effective and the couple stopped treating every person as beneath them, then it was worth it.

David strolled into the kitchen. Silence fell like an anvil. Even the food seemed reluctant to make a noise. He grinned at Connor. "I'm here to reprimand you for the way you spoke with the couple out front."

"Officially or unofficially?" Connor moved to the nearest stove and flipped a steak. His attention remained on the cast iron skillet.

David's grin spread. "Officially, I said I would talk with you. I never said what I'd say." He rocked back on his heels and shoved his hands into his pockets. "Next time they come in, get me right away, but you're not in any trouble."

A collective breath escaped the other employees, Jarrad included.

LATE THE NEXT MORNING, after Ellie's shift at the restaurant, Jarrad sat in her living room with a laptop on the coffee table. He tapped the screen and brought up a closer image of the bright yellow paint. "What about this one?"

Ellie scrunched her nose. "Too yellow."

"You've had an excuse for every color I've asked about." Jarrad leaned into the couch and folded his arms. "I'm beginning to think you don't know what you want."

"Maybe you have terrible taste in paint." Ellie popped the comment off quicker than a firecracker. Her gaze shuttered. "More like I'm scared out of my skin. Picking paint makes it real." Ellie scooted into the corner and brought one leg onto the cushion between them.

Jarrad chuckled. "Wait until you have to pay the first month's rent. Then it'll be real."

She groaned and brought her hands up to cover her face. "I want this. Really, I do. It's been my dream for years, but I can admit I'm absolutely terrified." Ellie peeked at him through her fingers. "Is that ridiculous?"

"No. That's human." Jarrad took one of her hands in both of his and squeezed. "I'd be worried if you were chill about this whole thing. It's a big deal. Huge." She groaned and he bit back a laugh. "But it's good, Ellie. This will work. If you build it, they will come."

Her groan turned into a laugh. "Did you just quote Field of Dreams at me?"

"I did. You recognized it though. What does that say about you?" He massaged her cold fingers and tapped the end of her nose. "Arnie's done with the building. I'm leaving in four hours. I don't want to be the spoil sport, but you need to make a decision."

"I'm never this uncertain." Her fingertips pecked his palm as she drummed them up and down. She faced the computer and chewed on her lip. "I like the blue, but half that street is blue. What about that?" She focused on the screen and leaned forward.

"Which one?" Jarrad leaned with her, bringing their faces closer together, where he could smell the ocean in her hair and feel a strand brush his cheek.

Ellie tapped. "That one." A sea-foam green popped onto the screen. Her brows lowered. "But I want a distressed look. We're sanding the whole place anyway. I like the wood look, but not for the whole building. So we distress it, like driftwood left in the sun. And we need wall decor. Nothing too cliche. Maybe a blackboard for the menu. Seashells around the border. Glass domes for the counter. The bottoms should be green and the tops clear. That'll make the colors in the food brighter."

"Glass covers for the counters. You don't want people touching the food."

Ellie nodded and he could see the moment when she caught the vision of what she wanted. It had been there the whole time. She'd just needed to bring it out to the light and make it real.

Two months and she'd show the world what Ellie Jones could do.

"I'm proud of you." Jarrad touched her shoulder.

She leaned into him. "I couldn't have done it without you."

He scoffed and she cuffed his shoulder with a light fist. "I mean it. You've helped more than you know. Not just helping with the contract and the building. Ruining the kitchen." She grinned a devious little smile. "You never made me feel like I can't do it or that it's a stupid idea."

Pride swelled up inside and puffed out his chest. He'd done what he set out to do. Convinced Ellie he was more than the kid she remembered. "It was my pleasure to help you. And to keep helping you."

He'd make it work somehow. Ellie couldn't pay him what he made at the Club Car. Or at the resort. His parents were paying him what they normally paid their cleaning crew, which was a decent amount more than might be typical. He earned every cent. "Have you told your parents yet?"

"I'm telling them tonight." She brushed her hair over her shoulder and tapped her lip. "What about the floors? Keep the hardwood, but do they need refinishing?"

Her sudden shift in topic told him she didn't want to talk about her parents. Or the potential disappointment she thought they'd feel. He understood. He'd gone through the same thing with his dad when he left for Nantucket.

"Your parents want what's best for you." He believed that, even of his own parents. They didn't show it well, but they wanted him to succeed. His dad just preferred his success come from the real estate business. Jarrad understood. The business was an empire his dad meant to pass down to his children. They'd heard the conversation a hundred different ways over the years. Olson Realty. His dad's pride and joy. A legacy in the making. A legacy his sister thrived on. Jarrad would happily let her take over.

Ellie's hands were on his arm, the pressure of her fingers digging into his tense muscles. She leaned her shoulder against his. "Are you nervous about going home?"

"No." Liar. He breathed through his nose, inhaling the scent of Ellie. "Yeah. Dad wasn't too happy when I skipped out to come here. I need to show him I'm making it work." A frown slipped out. "It's counter productive that I'm still working for them even though I'm living here. I wanted to be self-sufficient. Independent. That can't happen as long as they're still paying my bills. Even if I am earning the money."

"Hey." Ellie tapped his knee. "I work for my parents too. There's nothing wrong with that."

"You want to go walking on the beach?" He diverted the conversation, standing and tugging on her hand. "I need the sand between my toes one more time before I go back to the city and all the asphalt." He faked a shudder. "No green grass. No pink sunrises. It's all gray and blech."

Ellie's laugh rang out. Success. Two days in a row he'd made her laugh. She hooked her arm through his and waved at the door. "By all means, then. Let us take a stroll on the beach."

"You're sounding quite historical. Been watching Pride and Prejudice?"

She placed a palm on her chest and batted her lashes at him. "Why, Mr. Olson, whatever gave me away? Shall we take a stroll about the room? I'm quite sure we're causing a scandal being here without supervision. Should my father find out, you'll be forced to marry me."

Heat gathered at the base of his neck. "I'll tell the man myself." He tugged her toward the door. "Shall we head there straightaway?"

"Unhand me." Ellie started laughing hard enough her shoulders shook and tears ran down her cheeks. "You really do love movies."

"You sound surprised. It was one of the few things Dad and I never argued about. Old movies. Well. Old to me."

"Even Pride and Prejudice?"

"Well, the newer version with Keira Knightley is the only one we watched."

Ellie's laughter continued. "I'm not surprised. She has the tendency to draw in almost anyone."

"It's a good story." Jarrad held up a hand. "Don't ever ask me to read the book, because I refuse, but the movie was okay."

She nodded at the bookcases. "I have a confession to make. I've never read the book either. Most of the classics, really. Not my style." She turned and led the way out the door and down the steps while shaking her head and continuing to laugh.

What was her style? Jarrad mulled over everything he knew about Ellie as they stepped onto the sand. Wind and sand stung his legs and arms. The books he'd seen had bright colors, but he didn't catch any of the titles. He'd ask his sister, maybe stop by a bookstore on the mainland and see what he found that Ellie might like.

Chapter Eleven

ELLIE CALLED EVERY morsel of courage she possessed and held it close. Mom and Dad looked at each other, their faces showing traces of shock.

"When did you decide this?" Dad ruffled his hair and grimaced. "I thought you'd given up the idea of a bakery."

Never. She'd stopped talking about it when they kept coming up with reasons for her not to open. "Dad, this is my dream. What I've been working for all these years. You and Mom don't need me here, keeping the books. Not really."

"But, honey, you do such a wonderful job." Mom jumped into the conversation, her blue eyes wide.

Ellie smiled at her but shook her head. "And so will the next person. I need to do this. It's what I want."

"How are we supposed to find someone to replace you?" This came from Dad, who continued looking at Ellie like she'd asked to fly to the moon.

Really? She contained the frustrated sound tickling the back of her throat. They built the Rose Resort out of nothing and suddenly they had no idea how to find a new bookkeeper? "Ask Nathan. I'm sure there's a highschool kid who'd love a part-time job."

"Ellie—"

"Mom, I've made up my mind. I've signed the lease. I'll be painting and setting up next week." She reached out and grasped a hand from each parent. "Please be happy for me. You're entitled to your worry. I understand this is a big thing for me and a big change for you, but it's what I want. What I've always wanted."

Mom sniffled. Dad passed her his handkerchief and rubbed circles on her back. A single nod told Ellie he accepted. "I want what's best for you, kiddo. Always have. For all of you. If this is what you have to do, then do it. We're here to help if you need us. Ask, okay? Don't go it alone."

Point taken. He didn't like that she'd made so many moves ahead of the game without asking their opinion. It had been necessary, painful as it was to admit, to keep them in the dark until it was too late for them to talk her out of it.

"Why don't you come by Friday? I'll show you the space, and you can tell me what you think. Mom, I need your help with decorations." Ellie drew them into her plans with careful words. She did need her mom's help. The woman had single-handedly decorated the resort over the years. The climbing roses covering outside walls and giving the resort its name were her idea. She had more talent for decorating in her pinky than Ellie could dredge up in a hundred years. The ideas she'd given Jarrad were from her mother, years ago when they'd been able to discuss Ellie's bakery.

Put a piping bag or a recipe in her hand and she had creativity for days but present her with the blank canvas of an empty building and she faltered.

Not Jarrad. He'd come up with a hundred ideas in the space of an hour. They were off the wall and would never work, but he'd tried. Ellie stuffed thoughts of Jarrad back inside. He was on his way to the mainland and would be gone for the next two days. Her stomach churned. When he returned, they'd get to work.

How strange was it that they worked so well together? It was uncanny at how he understood her. How he made her laugh.

Dad tapped her knee and the quizzical look on his face warned her that he'd called her name at least once already. "I asked what time we should be there Friday."

"Oh. Um. Does seven sound okay?"

Mom answered with a pat to Dad's arm. "We'll be there. I'll bring my sketchbook and we'll talk. What colors are you going for?"

"Sea-foam for the walls and counters. Jarrad's picking it up for me while he's on the mainland."

Dad's eyebrows hiked upward at the mention of Jarrad's name. "Forgiven him, have you?"

Had she? Absolutely. The certainty of it settled deep inside. He'd changed, and so had she. They were learning to navigate friendship as adults. "He's not as bad as I thought. We're friends." She shrugged.

"Friends." Mom's voice lilted on a short laugh. "You sure that's all you are?"

She was so not discussing her love life with her parents. Sure, she'd kissed Jarrad. Twice. Neither time meant anything. Not to either of them. They were brief, in-the-moment, kisses and had nothing to do with romantic interest. Her heart protested with a painful thump. Ellie dismissed the feeling. She'd let herself feel too much for Jarrad already.

AT THE END OF HER SHIFT the next day, Ellie paused at the door when Connor called her name.

"Congratulations on the bakery." He twisted a towel in his hands and cleared his throat. "Can I take you to dinner? To celebrate." He rushed the last words, forcing her to concentrate to decipher them.

Dinner with Connor? She had plans with Jarrad when he came back. They were going to Slip 14. Her conversation from the day before interrupted. She and Jarrad were friends. Nothing more. Same with Connor. Friends could go to dinner. Connor never said it was a date. Did he mean it to be a date?

She nodded before the full implications of her feelings took over. "Dinner would be nice."

"Great." Connor broke into a smile that warmed Ellie with its brilliance. "I'll cook. Can we meet at your place, tonight around six?"

"My place?"

"Yeah. If you don't mind. I'll bring everything and clean up after, but it'll be easier to talk there. Get to know each other."

A chill swept down her spine. He meant a date. Like a real date in her house. "Sure." She tried not to think about how that one word twisted her insides into a hard knot. She liked Connor. He was a good guy. Solid. Dependable. Dinner with him was not a betrayal to Jarrad, who she was not dating but had only been working with . . . except for that one day they went to the lighthouse. Which wasn't a date. Dinner at Slip 14 was supposed to be an official date.

Why was she so confused?

She dialed Samantha while walking toward home. The phone rang twice before Samantha's breathless "Hello?" settled Ellie's nerves.

"You busy today?"

Papers rustled through the phone. "I can be done in an hour. What's up?"

Ellie breathed in, slow and purposeful, then filled Samantha in on the last few days. "I'm not sure if I'm doing the right thing."

"What? By having dinner with Connor?"

"Yes."

Samantha breathed a laugh through the phone. "You've not agreed to be exclusive with either of them. In fact, I'd say you really haven't even dated Jarrad. If you're this uncertain, ask. Ask Connor what his expectations are. Ask Jarrad the same thing. Then make up your mind. Who would you rather spend time with?"

"I don't know." The truth of that statement hurt in ways she didn't expect or anticipate. "They both have good qualities."

"Okay. You're not picking out a pet." More rustling papers. "I'll be at your house in a half hour. Think about what I said."

True to her word, Samantha burst through the front door right behind Ellie. She flung her arms around her cousin and squeezed. "I'm so confused."

"I noticed." Samantha hauled Ellie to the low couch and pushed her to a seated position. "You're overthinking this whole thing. What do you like about Jarrad?"

"He makes me laugh." And he believed in her. Pulled her from her negativity before it dragged her down.

Sam grinned. "That is part of his distinct charm. What about Connor?"

"He's steady and mature."

"Mm-hmm." Sam leaned into the corner and threw an arm over the back of the couch. "And who, my fun-loving, carefree cousin, would you rather spend the day with?"

"I don't know." Ellie slashed a hand through the air. "I've never spent time with Connor outside of work. I don't know what he's like when he's not in the kitchen."

"Will you find out tonight? He did agree to cook for you. That gets brownie points. But he'll still be in the kitchen, so will he act like he does at work or will you see the real Connor?" There was a sound of frustration in Samantha's voice that Ellie latched onto.

"You don't like Connor, do you? Because I'll call and tell him dinner's off if that's what you want."

Sam waved her hand and laughed. "No. Don't do that. It's work stuff that has me acting like a bear."

"Tell me. Maybe I can help." Ellie pressed for details. It was the least she could do since she always ran to Samantha for help. It felt nice to return the favor every once in a while.

By the time six rolled around, they'd discussed everything across Nantucket and Samantha's smile grew wider when Ellie stepped from the bedroom wearing a pink sundress and strappy sandals that showed off her legs and arms.

"You look great." Samantha gave Ellie a hug and backed away when a knock sounded on the door. "That's my cue to leave. Call me later." She winked and opened the front door. "Connor, glad to see you. If you'll excuse me, I'll get out of your way."

Connor stepped back with a glazed expression. He followed Samantha, turning his body as she walked down the steps. Finally, he cleared his throat and faced Ellie. "You look great." His tone was genuine.

Ellie flushed and held the door open. "Please, come in."

He followed her through to the kitchen, carrying two paper bags filled to the brim. After settling both bags on the kitchen table, he rubbed his hands together. "Now then. Sit back and relax while I take care of everything."

It was nice to have him in her kitchen. Her discomfort evaporated while he opened cabinets and drawers and removed the tools of his trade. Her kitchen became a haven of searing meat and fresh herbs. "What are you making?"

"Spicy chicken cacciatori." He swirled a spoon through a red sauce and faced her.

"Another of your grandmother's recipes?"

"Mine." His cheeks reddened.

"Anything I can do to help?" She felt a bit foolish sitting in her own kitchen doing nothing while he cooked. It was a generous gesture. She didn't deny that having Connor cook was a treat, but it felt wrong somehow for him to do all the work while she watched.

His smile returned even as he shook his head. "I want to do this for you. You deserve a break."

"So do you. You've been cooking all day. Don't you get tired of it?"

"Do you get tired of baking? Of creating new dishes and watching as people fall in love with the smell and flavor of your own creations?"

He had a point. "All right. You've convinced me." Ellie crossed her legs and relaxed with her glass of lemon water. Samantha's suggestion crept in. Ellie tightened her grip on the glass and eyed Connor. Should she ask now or wait until they sat down to eat?

"I'm glad you agreed to dinner." Connor looked up from his dishes and swallowed. "There's something I've been wanting to ask you. Now that we won't be working together."

Uh-oh.

He spooned chicken and sauce together and piled noodles onto two plates. After adding the sauce and a sprinkle of herbs, he carried both plates to the table and presented Ellie with one while lowering the other to the seat across from her.

"It smells wonderful." She only said the truth, but Connor's face lit up at her praise. The first bite burst with flavor. Spicy heat tickled the back of her throat. Ellie reached for her water. "Wow."

"Too much spice?" Connor took a bite and chewed with a thoughtful expression.

Ellie gulped a drink to cool her mouth. "Didn't expect it. Great flavor." She swirled another bite onto her fork and lifted it to her lips. "You said you wanted to ask me something."

"Are you and Jarrad dating?"

Ellie choked on a piece of chicken. Her throat tightened, cutting off her airflow. She coughed to clear it and shot a sliver of chicken across the table. A gasp worked its way out.

Connor dashed to her side. "Are you okay?"

Tears streamed from her eyes, but she nodded. The question caught her off guard. "Sorry," she croaked out. "Didn't expect you to ask that."

His frown pulled the skin around his mouth into deep crescents. "Is that a yes?"

"No." She managed to push the word through her burning throat. "Jarrad is helping me get the bakery set up. We went on one sort of date that I'm not sure was a date. Sort of like this one."

At that, Connor gaped at her. "You don't consider this a date?"

"I don't know. You asked if we could celebrate my opening the bakery. That doesn't say official date to me." She coughed into her napkin and reached for her water. The cool tang of lemon eased the last of the tightness from her throat. "I don't like lukewarm, maybe it is, maybe it isn't relationships. I prefer straightforward." And that's what was bothering her about Jarrad. Despite his obvious attraction, and hers, she had no idea how he felt about her. She wanted to know. Deserved to be told where he stood. And she needed to do the same. If only she knew where that was. The emotions going through her every time she thought about Jarrad and Connor were as shifting as the sands in the tide. When she thought she had hold of them, they moved.

It wasn't fair to any of them. Connor made her comfortable. Jarrad pushed her outside her comfort zone and made her laugh. Which was the better option and how did she decide?

"In that case." Connor settled onto the seat beside Ellie and gathered her hand to his chest. His palms warmed her and offered a sense of comfort. "Ellie, I've loved working with you. The only reason I didn't ask you out on a date before now was because we were co-workers. I didn't want to cross that line and create tension in the workplace. Since that isn't a problem anymore, would you go on a date with me on Friday?"

"I can't." Ellie sighed into her plate. "I'm showing my parents the building on Friday."

His gaze lifted from the table. "Saturday?"

"I'd like that." Her fingers twitched against Connor's chest as a new feeling blossomed. Seeing Connor happy made her happy. His smile was contagious.

He squeezed her hand, then released it and reached for his plate. "Tell me about your bakery. What are you going to call it?"

"Sweet by Design." The name tumbled from her lips. Should she keep it simple and personal and name it *Ellie's Bakery* instead? She had time to change her mind.

"It suits you—sweet." The corner of his lips turned upward.

Heat worked its way into her cheeks. She'd never expected Connor to have feelings for her. Or her for him. If that was what she could call it. Honestly, she felt confused more than anything. Connor was a talented chef who owned a rather impressive home on the beach. While she wouldn't love someone for their money, the stability gave her comfort.

Chapter Twelve

JARRAD STEPPED ONTO Nantucket soil and brought the briny air into his lungs. Home. No matter how many years he'd been gone, Nantucket worked its way into his heart and planted roots that could not be pulled loose. Even two days felt like an eternity away. Soon everything would be back to normal. An afternoon helping Ellie was all he needed to get settled again.

Nathan jogged across the small parking lot and waved at Jarrad. "Welcome home."

"Best place on earth." Jarrad grinned and reached for his bag. "The boxes for Ellie are right there." He hefted one into his arms while Nathan took the other.

"All this just for paint?" Nathan shook his head. "You got your eyes on my sister?"

What if he did? Jarrad sent a quiet look to Nathan's face and found mischief dancing in his friend's eyes. "She's finally warming up to me."

"Yeah? You and Connor both." Nathan juggled the box and pressed a button on his car remote. The trunk popped open. Nathan shoved the box inside and reached for the one in Jarrad's arms.

He tightened his grip. "What do you mean me and Connor both?" A knife in the gut would feel better than this sudden slicing pain that scorched both hot and cold.

Nathan gave him a look of sympathy. "She had a date with Connor. He cooked dinner at her house and they're going out again Saturday."

She was supposed to have a date with him Saturday. Right? Wait. He'd never set a day and time. Rookie move on his part, but why would she accept a date from another guy while agreeing to go out with him? "That makes no sense."

"You're telling me. I like Connor, but he's not right for Ellie. The two of them together is about as interesting as watching paint dry."

"Hey, even that can be fun if you're with the right person." He'd looked forward to sitting with her and chatting between coats of paint. He'd imagined a cozy afternoon with coffee and sandwiches. Maybe a paint fight. Ellie would look cute brandishing a paintbrush at him like a sword. Maybe he'd even prove himself to be a Wesley. All those hopes flew away on seagull wings. Jarrad shook his head to banish the thoughts. "We should get this stuff to the resort. Ellie's picking it up there." And he could see her. Talk to her and find out what she was thinking.

Nathan chattered about his school kids during the short drive. Jarrad commented when necessary but spent most of the time working out what to say to Ellie. He worked alongside Nathan to unload the boxes of paint, leaving them in the storage closet. A wave of memories crashed in as the door opened without a sound. Working here with Ellie was one of his favorite moments. She'd started to loosen up and believe in him.

Samantha clipped down the hallway, her heels popping with every step. She paused at the open door. "I'm glad I caught you two. Jarrad, Margaret wants you to go through Unit 16 again. There's a couple coming in this afternoon and they're sticklers for cleanliness." Samantha leaned against the frame and sighed. "How did I get roped into this?"

"Can't answer that." Nathan picked up a can of paint and spun it around to read the color. He cast a look at Jarrad. "Where's Ellie?"

"Out with Connor. He asked her to go sailing."

Sailing? Jarrad's hopes plummeted. Connor had his own boat. Something Jarrad could never afford. His dad owned a nice speedboat but asking for the keys to it would be akin to agreeing to come back to the mainland for eternity. Not happening. For someone who claimed not to have time for a social life or a relationship, Ellie seemed to be making do just fine the minute he left Nantucket.

Nathan dusted off his hands and moved to the door. "I'm out of here."

"That reminds me. Steve needs you in the office. Something about interviewing for Ellie's position." Samantha rolled her hands in circles and pushed off from the door. A look of concern flitted across her face when she locked eyes with Jarrad. "You really like her." A statement that had Nathan turning their way instead of leaving the room to attend to resort business with his dad.

"You should tell her." Nathan threw his two cents into the ring, unwanted but genuine.

Knowing Nathan supported Jarrad in his pursuit emboldened him. "I won't interfere with her decision. If she liked me half as much as I thought she did, she'd never have agreed to a date with Connor. She can make up her own mind who she wants to spend her time with."

"It's my fault she's seeing him." Samantha's voice was low, the tone pleading. "Don't blame Ellie. She didn't know what to do. I convinced her to give Connor a chance and see who she liked more." She winced. "That sounds terrible. I didn't mean for you to get hurt. Ellie's trying to figure out what's best for her."

"You mean who's best for her." Jarrad tried to keep his tone discreet, but it came out sharp and cold. Ellie had every right to date whomever she wanted. He pushed a hand through his hair and paced the small room.

Nathan slipped out with an apology that hardly sounded genuine. None of it mattered.

"For what it's worth, she really likes you." Samantha stayed in the doorway but began to back away when Margaret called her name from the front of the building. "Don't give up."

This coming from the woman who told Ellie it was okay to date both men at the same time? Classic. He'd never taken Samantha for the type to encourage Ellie in the dating game.

Jarrad edged his frustration aside. He did not have a right to be angry. He and Ellie did not have an exclusive relationship. One date did not a relationship make. He needed a plan to show Ellie how he felt about her. Something she couldn't resist. It was that or give up, and he'd never been a quitter.

THE FOLLOWING AFTERNOON, after Ellie's shift and before his began, Jarrad knocked on the door of Ellie's bakery and forced out a carefree smile when she swung it open. "Mind if I help?" He'd spent the day before sanding every square inch of the place. The guy he'd hired called in sick and rather than put Ellie behind schedule, he did the work himself.

Every muscle ached and lifting his arms over his head made him want to curl into a ball and never move again, but it was worth the smile on her face when she waved a hand at him now and pulled him inside. "This looks great. I was sure one person would never get the work done in time, but your guy pulled through."

"About that." He waited until he had her full attention. "I did it."

Ellie's nose wrinkled. "Did what?"

"The guy couldn't make it. I stayed most of the night to get it done."

Her gasp and the hand she threw to her mouth made every ache worthwhile. He'd wanted to prove something to her, and this was one way to get straight to the heart of the matter. "I didn't want you to be disappointed."

"Jarrad. You didn't have to do that. You could have waited. Or called me. I would've helped." She threw her arms around him and squeezed tight.

His thoughts turned into darting fish that scattered before he could catch one and bring it to the surface. "Happy to help. And when I'm working here, you won't have to worry about a thing."

Her arms slid away, and she backed up a step. "About that."

Now what?

"I don't think I can hire you."

"I thought we already agreed it was a done deal." They had, hadn't they? He'd asked Connor to change his shifts. Connor. Jarrad's teeth clenched. "Did Connor tell you it was a bad idea?"

"No." Ellie shook her head, sending hair flying. She scooped it into a ponytail and concentrated on opening a can of paint. The metal pail resisted her efforts. She grunted and banged on the lid.

Even her grunts were cute. Jarrad pulled the can away and pried the lid off with a flip of the screwdriver. "So why can't you hire me? We work great together."

"I can't afford to pay you what you're worth." She slid her gaze away from him. "Mom has this friend whose daughter needs a job. She's taking college classes online and needs a job in the early morning. It's perfect for her, and you can keep your jobs. You won't have to take a paycut."

"Is this really about money? Is it because I don't make enough money that you're backing away from me and dating Connor?"

Ellie's gasp shot a bolt of lightning into his stomach. He'd not meant to say that.

"I'm sorry. That was petty. I just don't understand." He understood that two day's absence left the door open to Connor's machinations and Ellie leaped at the chance to go out with the man. Who wouldn't? He was smart, successful, rich. All the things Jarrad had yet to accomplish. Was that why Ellie pulled away? He despised feeling this way, like he wasn't good enough. What else was he to think though?

"No. You're right. I did make it sound like you're working here was a sure thing. Is that really what you want though? You'll be working for a fraction of the money and the hours are terrible." She held a hand to her chest. "Trust me. I've done it for years. It's not worth it. You're better off staying where you are and getting paid what you're worth."

Which meant he'd have no time to spend with her. Their shifts would always clash. He could open his own place, but that wouldn't solve the problem either.

"I got you something." Ellie stood and darted behind the counter. For several minutes, she rummaged around. Metal scraped the floor in a nails-on-chalkboard whine that cut through the air.

The stench of paint drowned out the last of the musty aroma inside the small building. Jarrad scanned the space. Nothing had changed since he left at dawn. Same bare-wood counters, dinged up from years of use. Same spotty ceiling. He made a mental note to call a roofer to check for water damage.

Ellie emerged with her hands behind her back and a cheeky grin complimenting her blue eyes. Her steps crackled on the plastic spread out to protect the floor from paint. She brought her right arm out and flourished a book. "Here." She pushed it toward him.

Jarrad read the title. "One hundred and one pranks for the unsuspecting." He flipped it open to the first page. "Let the air out of your boss' tires so he's stuck at work." If Connor drove to work, he might be tempted.

"I thought you'd like this one." Ellie pointed to a dog-eared page.

He flipped to the bent edge. "Sabotage a package of Oreos by scraping out the cream and replacing it with toothpaste." He read the rest of the page and started to laugh. "I've done a few of these. Thanks, Ellie." He wrapped an arm around her shoulders and brought her close. "These are great."

"Don't prank me. If you do, I'll know it was you." She wagged a finger at him, scolding with her tone like they were back to being teenagers.

He held up a hand. "I promise I won't prank you with anything I find in this book." Anything he thought up on his own, however, was fair game. And she never said he couldn't prank everyone else with the ideas she'd given him.

"Good. Now." She slapped her palms together and rubbed. "I'm ready to paint. Shelves first." With a long look at him, she rolled her shoulders. "I appreciate your help, but you don't have to stay if you're too tired."

"Are you kidding? I've been looking forward to this all day." It was the truth, and it caused Ellie to smile his favorite smile.

She flipped her phone onto a music app and let the sound ease into the room. Debussy. He wasn't the least bit surprised.

"You want me to get the top shelves?"

Ellie nodded her head and moved to the rhythmic tune with her eyes closed. He considered making a smart remark about painting with her eyes closed but held it in. The perfect peace on her face drew him to silence. She was perfectly content here with him in this moment. He treasured it, her ability to be at ease with him.

He'd never take her acceptance for granted.

Jarrad stirred the can of paint before pouring it into a tray. He turned back for the ladder.

Paint slurped in the unmistakable sound of a roller going up and down the tray. Suddenly, a swipe of cold ran up his arm and Ellie giggled.

He twisted his arm around and sure enough, a trail of green ran from his elbow to the cuff of his shirt. "You are in so much trouble."

Ellie waved the roller at him. "That's payback. Now we're even."

"Not even close." He snatched a clean brush from the pack at his feet and ran it through the paint. "We can do this the easy way, or the hard way."

"Hmm. Let me think." Ellie slashed the air, connecting the roller with his chin before he could react.

"Game on." He lunged and caught her elbow. Her shriek threatened to split his eardrums, but he hauled her in and patted the brush along the back of her neck. "You look good in green. Maybe we can turn you into a mermaid." A glob of paint fell from his brush and dripped down her leg. "Oh look, we're already on our way."

This time, the roller ran up his cheek and into his hair. Laughter rang out over the music, lifting the cold from his chest and filling it with heat. She should always laugh like this. With complete abandon and joy. It charged the room with happiness and made his day brighter.

He growled with pretend annoyance and let her go to wipe his hand over his face. The action spread the paint but also gave him green fingers, which he wiggled in her direction. "Come here, my pretty, and get your just rewards."

"You first." Ellie grabbed a brush and scooped paint onto the bristles. Paint splattered the plastic with the patter of raindrops.

Jarrad advanced while holding his brush and hand in front of him. He hit a large paint drop and slid. His right leg went forward and put him into a lunge. He swiped at Ellie's arm, but she leaped away, spun on her heel, and came back at him with her dual weapons. He took a roller to the stomach and a brush across his forehead before his balance faltered. The ground rushed up to meet his back with a heavy thud that knocked his breath from his lungs and the brush from his hand.

He tried to laugh. Or move.

Ellie fell beside him and planted a hand on his chest. Her face came into focus as he hauled in a breath. Paint coated the ends of her hair and brushed over his neck with a wet sensation. He'd never seen a more beautiful woman than Ellie with paint stripes on her face and a smile that rivaled the heavens bursting open at sunrise.

This moment. Her, here with him, with laughter dimpling her cheeks, was the happiest moment of his life.

Her laughter quieted as she scanned his face. A pulse jumped in her throat, a rapid flutter that matched his own. He glanced at her lips now pulled in a side pout and was a heartbeat away from kissing her when he remembered. She had a date with Connor. Reality hit colder than water from the Arctic. Jarrad closed his eyes and thumped the floor with the back of his head.

Ellie pushed against his chest and the sound of her rising to her feet steadied his breaths. He could do this. He had no choice. Opening his eyes, Jarrad rolled to his feet and picked up the paint tray. He didn't bother cleaning the paint from his skin, clothes, or hair. None of it mattered.

What mattered was getting this job done.

Chapter Thirteen

THERE WAS A GOOD CHANCE she'd made a mistake. Ellie couldn't get the night of the paint fight with Jarrad out of her head. Every time she walked into her bakery, she flashed back to the hours they spent goofing around instead of working. For every swipe of paint across the counters, there had been a splatter on the floor. Thank goodness she'd covered every bit of the hardwood with plastic, or it would look like some kind of Picasso.

Giving him the joke book was a definite blunder. What possessed her to give the king of pranks ammunition? When she found it on her shelf while rearranging her rom coms, it had felt like a good idea. She bought it years ago, back when Jarrad visited every summer and made her life miserable, with every intention of paying him back for his pranks.

Too late to take it back.

Just like it was too late to back out of her date with Connor tonight.

Ellie took one last look in the mirror and cleaned a spot of lipstick from her teeth. She'd taken care with her appearance and opted to wear her favorite, a bohemian dress that swirled around her ankles and made her want to twirl.

Connor had been silent on where they were going but assured her that a dress and low heels were appropriate.

Her phone rang, startling Ellie from her stare into the mirror.

Connor.

She swiped the phone from the table. Her stomach tumbled. "Hello?"

"Hey, Ellie, I'm going to be a little late." Connor's voice held a hint of frustration, a tone she recognized from working with him at the restaurant. His footsteps echoed through the phone with heavy thuds.

"Are you okay?" The whirling sensation in her belly went haywire. She pressed a hand to her middle.

A sigh, then, "Yeah, I'm fine. Car trouble. Someone let all the air out of my tires."

"That's terrible."

"Tell me about it." Another set of stomping steps and a mutter of voices she couldn't distinguish. "I'm getting it fixed now. Can you give me a half hour?"

"Sure." She nodded out of habit and paced to the couch where she flopped with the phone pressed to her ear. "Who would do something like that?"

"No idea. I'm just grateful they didn't do anything serious like slash the tires. This feels like a teenage prank, something a kid would do. Or payback for something. I could see Mrs. Townsend sending her son to prank me, but how would they know where I live? They're not local."

She'd heard all about his encounter with the exasperating couple. But this seemed petty, even for them. Who would bother to prank Connor?

Jarrad.

Ellie lifted a palm to her forehead. That book. He'd read from it the night they painted together, and the first thing was letting the air out of people's tires.

Oh, she was going to pay him back for this. How juvenile. He knew she had a date with Connor tonight. No doubt he'd done this on purpose to try and ruin her night. He'd been petty when they were kids, and it looked like his attitude hadn't changed.

"Ellie?"

"I'm here. Sorry. I was thinking."

Connor chuckled. "I said I'll be there soon as I can."

"I'll be waiting." They said goodbye and Ellie ended the call. Seconds later, she had a search pulled up and a list of pranks to read through. She needed the perfect idea. Simple but unpredictable. A prank Jarrad would never see coming or suspect she was behind. Most were too invasive for her tastes and required tons of setup. Like sneaking into his house and stealing all the sheets. Or sabotaging all the food in the refrigerator. He'd definitely know that was her after the episode in her building.

What to do? What to do?

Ellie continued reading and scrolling until the knock on her door signaled Connor's arrival. She met him with a smile.

Connor matched her grin and waved an arm. For someone who'd been pranked, he appeared calm and not the least bit disturbed. "Shall we?"

"We shall." Ellie approached Connor's car and slid into the passenger seat. "Where are we going?"

"Keepers Restaurant. I've been dying to check out their menu and see how it compares to what we're doing at the Club Car." Connor gripped the wheel, and a gleam entered his eyes.

Well that wasn't romantic at all. Ellie resisted the urge to cross her arms and fall into melancholy over the fact that Connor didn't intent to treat this like a date so much as an audition for the competition. Disappointment settled deep, and she forced it away before her face revealed the emotion.

Connor prattled on about the menu, listing Keepers dishes like they were exquisite wines and expounding on how he could make them better.

She nodded from time to time but didn't speak. This side of Connor had never shown itself, and she didn't know what to think of this side of his personality. He wasn't frightening or boring so much as intense and well, yes, boring.

Was this how people felt when she talked about the bakery? Surely not. It wasn't like she talked about nothing else.

"Have you ever been to the whaling museum?" Ellie interjected after a solid minute of Connor's monologue.

He glanced at her. "No. I spend most of my free time checking out the other restaurants. There are over eighty of them, so it takes a while to get through the list. By the time I visit the last one, it's time to start over again and try something new from each menu."

"Sounds . . . exhausting." Thinking about it made her head ache. Would she feel that way after her bakery opened? Like she had to compete with every single other business? No. She refused.

Connor steered them into the parking lot, still talking about a Cobb salad he'd eaten and the wilted lettuce.

What happened to the guy who cooked her dinner and carried on a normal conversation?

Ellie escaped from the car and hurried to the building where they were shown to a square table next to a row of windows that offered a view of the outside world.

"I'd hoped to get a booth," Connor said as he slid onto his seat across from her. "Looks like they're all full. Is this okay?"

"It's fine." Ellie lowered her napkin to her lap and cupped her chin in her palm with her elbow on the table. Not her best manners, but did it matter at this point? She had a gorgeous view over Connor's shoulder if he slipped back into his restaurant tirade. "What made you want to be a chef?" Ellie worked to steer the conversation to a palatable subject.

Connor froze with his napkin in his hand. His expression crumpled. "I did it again, didn't I?"

"What?"

"Ranted about food. Restaurants. The whole bit." Connor shook his head and reached over the table to grasp her fingers. "I'm sorry. I get obsessed with work sometimes. You can tell me when I've crossed the line. My family does it all the time."

Relief pushed out the disappointment and lifted Ellie's spirits. "It's okay. I get it. I think I could talk about the bakery for hours and hours."

"But you don't want to feel like you're boring everyone else. I get it." Connor pressed his fingers into her wrist then let go. "No more talk of menus, unless you ask me a question. I can tell you all about this place, but they do have a new item I might try."

Ellie let the room's ambiance settle around them. This was the Connor she'd come to know and respect. Their waiter returned, and Ellie ordered the burger sliders while Connor rattled off an order too complex to follow. "I don't mind talking about food. What's your favorite dish to cook?"

"Pass." Connor wiggled his eyebrows and leaned into his seat. "Let's talk about you. When did you know you wanted to open a bakery?"

"When I got my first Easy Bake oven for Christmas. I was six. Baking was magical. You take these random ingredients, and you turn them into a confectionery delight. It wasn't until I made Katrina's wedding cake that it really hit me that I could do it. I could open a bakery of my own and spend every day baking and decorating."

"You want to make wedding cakes all the time or is that a low priority?"

Ellie fiddled with her napkin and sipped her water before answering. "In the middle. I love wedding cakes but the stress that comes with them isn't my favorite. I like making people happy, and I can do that with a slice of pie in the afternoon or a baguette on the way to work."

"And Jarrad is helping you accomplish this?" The words were spoken carefully, without inflection, but a look at Connor's face showed tension framing his eyes. Curiosity or jealousy?

Ellie had no frame of reference to help her understand the subtleness of the look. "Jarrad has been a good friend who's done everything possible to get me started."

"He came to me and asked to switch shifts. I'm assuming so he can work with you."

Her head moved side to side. "It's best if we don't work together." It wasn't wrong for her to admit that to Connor, was it? Jarrad already knew, but what if he'd asked for a different shift for some other reason? "But you should ask him about it."

"Are you dating him?" Connor winced and rubbed his forehead. "Forget I asked. You don't have to answer, it's just . . . I like you, Ellie. I have for a long time, and I want to give this a shot. You and me. We make a great team, and we understand the stress the other is under in the food business. It's a mutually beneficial relationship."

And not the least bit romantic when explained that way. Ellie was saved from answering by the arrival of their food. As the dark-haired man lowered her plate to the table, a clatter rang out from the kitchen area. Connor's head jerked up. For a moment, Ellie thought he would rush away to investigate the noise.

"Please, do not worry yourselves. It's James, our newest employee. He forgets to call out when he's walking behind someone in the kitchen. That's the third time this week he's dropped a tray." Their waiter, whose apron was stitched with the name Todd in silver thread, shook his head but managed a short laugh. "We've been giving him non-breakable items to practice. Sounds like it isn't helping."

"Will he be fired?" Connor leaned his elbows on the table and focused on Todd.

"I don't know." He inclined his head. "Please, enjoy your meal." He threaded his way through the crowded room and disappeared into the kitchen.

Chatter from the surrounding tables resumed. Ellie picked up her first slider and took a bite. Juicy hamburger and sharp cheddar sang a melody across her taste buds.

Connor worked a bite toward his mouth, chewed, and swallowed. He nodded. "Almost perfect. I can't place the spice they're using."

Ellie let the food talk for her to keep from answering Connor's last question. A question she had no honest way of knowing the answer to.

SHE WAITED UNTIL AFTER Connor dropped her off to put her plan into motion. Retribution was in her hands, and justice would be swift. All without Jarrad realizing she was the instigator behind the prank.

A bag of sand and a block of charcoal later, she was peddling her bicycle to Jarrad's little house while the night wind teased her hair. Katydids sang from the bushes. Ellie kept peddling. With her mind focused on the task at hand, she was able to ignore the creepy crawlies that sent shudders down her spine and goosebumps across her arms.

Jarrad's bungalow popped into view and Ellie coasted to a stop. No sounds came from inside the house and every window remained dark. They'd agreed to meet the next morning to continue work on the building. Hopefully that meant he was sound asleep and wouldn't wake if she made a few quiet noises. Like laughing.

Ellie ran in a crouch down the sandy walkway and ducked behind the house. Jarrad's bicycle rested against a wall with no chain or device to keep anyone from taking it. She considered moving it, but her ideas were better if he suspected nothing.

A light flicked on inside. Ellie dove into a bush and covered her mouth with both hands to keep laughter from spilling out. A katydid screamed in her ear, and it took every shred of self-control to keep from screaming. Her breaths came out in pants as noises from inside the house seeped through the walls. The kitchen faucet turned on, then the house went dark. Ellie waited, counting to ten before she crept from the bush.

She worked quick and silent, smearing charcoal all along the inside of his helmet so that when he wore it the next morning, he'd have a line of soot around his head. The sand she poured onto the seat, hoping that when he sat it would be too dark to notice the fine grains. It wouldn't be until he set off down the road that the particles worked their way into his clothes.

If she had itching powder, she'd put that on the handlebars, but since she didn't, a rub of hot pepper flakes did the trick. One swipe across his eyes and they'd be tearing up. She chuckled all the way home as she imagined seeing him. It would take serious acting to keep her face straight tomorrow, but for tonight she enjoyed the thrill of adrenaline spiking her heartbeat.

Now she understood what he got out of it all those years ago. If he'd brought it down a notch, she might have found them funny. None of the things he'd experience would hurt him. Annoy and irritate, yes, but not hurt.

She'd been right to back away from Jarrad. The juvenile behavior was fun in small doses, but she wanted a relationship with a man who knew the ins and outs of life, not who wondered how many pranks he could pull on the same person before they figured out the culprit. A man like Connor. He might have a tendency to ramble about food and obsess over his competition, but he also knew how to switch that off and be a caring partner.

Ellie imagined trying to prank Connor and came up empty. Nothing would be funny to him unless it happened to someone else, and certainly not in the kitchen. He'd take offense to his domain becoming a playground. Yet another reason for Ellie to keep Jarrad out of the bakery once it opened. He'd not think twice about switching the sugar with salt and ruining countless recipes if it gave him a chance to laugh.

Chapter Fourteen

JARRAD SWIPED A HAND over his forehead, and the stinging in his eyes increased. What was going on? An itch started on the back of his left thigh. He let go of the handlebars and scratched. Sand came away under his fingernails. He focused his bleary gaze on the road and blinked to clear the tears trickling from his eyes. His nose started to run.

He didn't feel sick. Other than the stinging eyes and drippy nose, he felt normal. And the itching. What was that all about?

Wheeling into town, he stopped at The Coffee Grind and picked up his and Ellie's order. He took off his helmet before going inside and used the back of his hand to wipe his forehead.

A woman passed by and raised her eyebrows after giving him a quick look. Jarrad hurried into the coffee shop and snatched the paper cups from the white counter.

"Hey, Jarrad." Katie shouted at him from across the room. The petite woman took his order every morning and had it ready for him to pick up. She pressed a button on one of the massive machines and slid between two other women to meet him at the corner. Her eyes widened. "You okay?"

"Fine."

"Uh-huh. You got a little something—" She waved at her forehead. "Here."

A towel was shoved into his face, the quick swipes scraping the sweat from his skin.

Katie frowned. "Did you dye your hair?"

"No. Why?"

"You're covered in black."

What? That couldn't be right. He'd showered this morning and even glanced in the mirror before leaving, even though he didn't style his hair. Why bother when the helmet flattened it?

Katie showed him the towel, where a streak of black covered the tan material. "There's more on your forehead. It doesn't want to come off."

Great. He knew now why the woman looked at him like he'd grown a second head. He gave Katie a tight grin. "Thanks for telling me. I'll take care of it." He sauntered out of the shop and set the coffees on a nearby bench before reaching for his helmet. Tilting it to the sun, he caught a glimpse of black powder ground into the hard plastic.

He ran a finger around the rim, and it came away black. Paint? No. Too grainy. Jarrad sniffed the helmet. Charcoal. He knew that burnt smell. Why hadn't he noticed when he strapped it on at home?

That explained the problem with his head, but what about his eyes, nose, and the constant itching on his rear? Jarrad risked letting the coffee go cold and examined the bike from handlebars to wheels. His nose dripped, and he swiped the back of his hand over it, sending a wave of heat into his eyes.

"Pepper." A laugh gusted out. Someone pranked him by sabotaging his bicycle. A someone who knew he'd be riding soon. Jarrad picked up the coffees and straddled the seat. He steered with one hand and held the tray with the other. A couple years as a bike deliveryman helped him maintain his balance, and he arrived at Ellie's bakery unscathed except for the continued burning.

She met him at the door, her eyes growing wide as she took in his face. A hand lifted to her mouth. "What happened to you?"

"You tell me." Jarrad handed her the coffee. He should have figured it out sooner and done something to her coffee as payback. Ellie was responsible for his miserable state. He knew that as well as he knew his own name. She made sense as the perpetrator. But why?

Had she started to miss his pranks? A hundred different ideas cascaded into his mind at once. So many pranks. So little time. One stood out from the rest, and he handed her the coffee to free his hands.

"I . . . I don't know what you're talking about." Her gaze slid away, a giggle slipping out. Ellie spun on her heel and dashed into the building, leaving him holding the bicycle while tears continued tracking down his face.

He stowed the bike and helmet and followed her inside, where he strolled into the kitchen and turned on the faucet and stuck his head under the rush of water. Blessed relief. A rag touched his hand, the rough texture perfect for removing the charcoal. He worked fast to clean up and scrubbed his hands with a bar of soap Ellie nudged his way.

Her form was a blurry blob from the combination of pepper and water, but Jarrad let his gaze roam her face. When she thought he wasn't looking, a grin emerged.

Guilty. She might as well have stamped it across her forehead.

Two could play this game. And he had more practice at being an unknown threat that people never saw coming or suspected later.

"How was your date with Connor?" The words tasted sour on his tongue. He'd intended to take Ellie on a date, but now she was seeing Connor, he refused. No way he'd be part of some round robin dating project. Not even for Ellie.

Ellie stiffened and crossed her arms. Interesting. Either the date went horribly wrong, or she didn't like him asking about it. Or both. "Fine." Her tone said otherwise.

Jarrad let it go, nodding his head and drying off his face. He buried his head in the towel and took his first clear breath since leaving home this morning. Was that? Did he smell bread? He sniffed again without the towel blocking his nose. Yeasty goodness. "What are you baking?" He looked around. Still no oven. "Or what did you bake and bring with you?"

"Cinnamon rolls." Ellie scuffed her toe on the linoleum and put a palm to her cheek. "After Samantha's gushing, I thought I'd give them a try. You want one?"

He did, but what if she'd pranked them too. Jarrad let his excitement show so Ellie wouldn't suspect anything and tossed the towel on the counter. "I wouldn't say no to that."

Ellie retrieved a box from under the newly painted counter and presented it to him with a broad smile. Hmm. Suspicious.

"Don't you want one?" He peeked into the box. They smelled divine, but he waited. Six round pastries covered with gooey icing. Would Ellie ruin an entire recipe to ensure he took a bad one? He wouldn't put it past her after this morning.

"I ate two already." She nudged the box closer to his waiting fingers. "Go ahead, they won't bite."

"I don't think I'm hungry." His stomach cramped at the blasphemous words. He was near starving, but he didn't want any part of Ellie's prank. But if they were not sabotaged, he was missing out on a delicious breakfast. And if they were, then he had cause to prank her back.

What a dilemma.

Ellie started to pull the box away and a frown creased her face as her eyes lowered. "Well, they're here if you change your mind." She returned the box to the nook and brushed off her hands. "What are we working on today?"

"The roof guy is coming tomorrow. Floors and walls are done. You have your boxes and decorations ordered?"

A nod. "They'll start arriving on tomorrow's plane, but I should have everything by the end of next week. I took Mom's advice on the décor, and I'm having them shipped here." She motioned at the room around them.

Boxes. Shipments. An idea formed. A prank that even Ellie couldn't hate. Jarrad snapped his expression into obedience before he gave away his glee. He forced his voice to remain neutral. "Let's work in the kitchen today. Appliances are scheduled for Tuesday. You have your employees lined up?" That question hurt, but he asked anyway. His job here was to get her business up and running. If he could manage to keep his personal feelings out of the way.

"Most of them." Her tone was subdued. "Look, Jarrad—"

"Don't worry about it." If he heard her excuses, it would only make things worse. She didn't trust him to work with her. Not when it really mattered. Not in the day-to-day operations where his real skills came into play. Knowing that she found him incapable of the job sent the coffee in his stomach to roiling. He'd intended to prove himself to Ellie. If he couldn't even do that, then why not act like the juvenile she already expected?

One prank. Coming right up. While Ellie went to work scrubbing the floors and counters, he took a few minutes to tap on his phone. That's all he needed to put the wheels in motion. On the off chance the cinnamon rolls were legit, he grabbed one and sank his teeth into the soft dough. Cinnamon and sugar goodness with just the right amount of crisp to the outer edges. It almost made him want to cancel the order on its way to Ellie's front door. Almost.

ELLIE RAN TO THE FRONT door and met Stan the mailman before he parked the truck. She all but clapped her hands when he started hauling boxes to her building. She put the bakery's address on the orders, just because she could. It felt right to have all the decorations arrive here.

He laughed at her glee. "Been waiting on these, I take it."

"You have no idea." A lifetime of waiting. Or the equivalent of almost twenty years. What she remembered of her lifetime. The realization of a dream. That was what those packages represented. She took the first one from him and hauled it into what would be the dining area.

Tables and chairs were the last thing to arrive. Mere days before she was scheduled to open. Her stomach gave a heave. They were pushing to get it all done in time, but she had faith that Jarrad would pull through.

Her prank worked better than she expected and had been worth every second of nail-biting to keep from laughing. He'd looked shocked and confused but still managed to appear confident. He seemed to have no idea who did it, and he hadn't even brought it up the whole day.

Did things like that happen to him so often that he couldn't muster up any feelings about it?

"Last one." Stan rolled an enormous box into the room on his hand cart and lowered it to the floor. "Looks like a good one. Early Christmas for you." He scratched at his head under the brim of his hat and peered around the room. "Whatcha building?"

"Bakery." Ellie grunted as she slid a trio of boxes into a line. "And you get a free cup of coffee every time you deliver my mail. Once I get the machines hooked up. They should be here next month."

"Hope I'm not the one delivering that." Stan grimaced and massaged his back. "Did that for The Coffee Grind. Threw my back out for a week."

Who would deliver the larger packages? The appliances were coming from a place on the mainland. Her coffee machine wasn't that big. She needed to check the description again.

"Well, I'm out of here. Good to see you, Ellie. Can't wait to pop in for a slice of pie."

He was out the door before she could tell him she might not have pie. Oh well. With no one around to see, Ellie rubbed her palms together and bounced on her toes. What a great day. And it was barely two. Her shifts at the Club Car were still exhausting, but this made every minute worthwhile.

She sat on the floor and pulled the first box close. The label indicated it came from the glass company she'd ordered the cake plates from. Her hands itched to see the green glass atop the freshly painted counters.

A swipe of the boxcutter over the tape and she was in. Styrofoam packages ensconced the glass and took her several minutes to unearth the fragile material. Soft green with clear domes. Ellie held the dome to the light and grinned as it refracted and sent arcs of color around the walls.

The second box was stuffed with wall décor. Things her mom recommended, and Ellie had ordered without really looking except to make sure it was within her budget. She ran her fingers over the gilt-framed mirror that would hang behind the counter.

She didn't recognize the logo on the next box, but at this point she had put in so many orders they were all starting to blur together. Her list. Ellie fumbled for her phone and cross checked the items on her list from the day's arrivals.

A checkmark beside each item so she didn't lose her mind trying to remember later and she was ready to open the dented box with the weird label.

Ellie spun it around, looking for any identifying marks but found plain cardboard on all sides. Huh. She raised onto her knees to reach the top of the box and sliced through the tape. A pop sounded from within the box and the flaps exploded outward. Ellie caught a flash of color before it blew into her face with a flurry of sound and the sensation of a million grains of sand pelting her skin.

What. Was. That?

Her eyes closed, then opened. Sparkles of pink. Everywhere. The floor was covered in glitter. And her face. Ellie blinked and scrunched her cheeks, feeling the pinch of the tiny dots. Every blink dislodged a shower of pink into her lap. Even her eyelashes were coated and so *heavy.* How did women stand those fake eyelashes? The flecks of pink weighed hers down until blinking became a chore.

"Hey, Ellie, I got done early at work and—" the feminine voice cut off.

Ellie turned. A shower of glitter rained down from her hair. Samantha stood in the doorway with both hands over her mouth. No wonder people said they resembled each other. They had that look in common. Utter shock.

Samantha took a step and lowered her hands. "What happened?"

Her brain stopped working when the glitter hit. Even now she struggled to put anything into words. One stood out and pounded the back of her head. "Jarrad." He'd figured it out. He knew she was responsible for his misery yesterday. And this was payback.

"But why?" Samantha tried to school her expression, but a smile slipped out, along with a laugh before she coughed and cleared her throat. "I'm sorry. You look like a mad fairy." She wrapped her hands around her middle and guffawed.

Ellie continued to blink glitter. She pushed to her feet and dusted off but only succeeded in sending a patter of glitter to the floor. Cleaning up would take ages. And she'd be finding glitter for the next ten years. Ellie started to turn but caught her reflection in the mirror.

Sam's assessment was on hundred percent on point. Mad fairy indeed.

Let the games begin. If he wanted a prank war, he'd get a prank war.

"Sam, I need you to put your brain to work and come up with a payback prank."

"Why not you?" Sam asked between gasps.

Ellie shook her hands. "Because my brain seems to be on vacation right now and all I can think of is stomping over to the restaurant and throwing glitter in his face. I want subtle but unforgettable. This means war."

Her cousin's laughter cut off. "Are you sure? Jarrad is a good guy, but he can get carried away. I don't want this going too far. You two were just starting to like each other."

"I'm sure. It's time someone taught him a lesson. And I'll be his instructor."

"You want him to know it was you?"

Ellie nodded then reached up to shake glitter from her hair. "I'm never getting rid of this."

"Go home and take a shower. I'll start cleaning up here." Samantha took Ellie's arm and led her to the door.

"I can't go through town looking like this."

"I love you, Ells, but you're not getting in a car like that. Maybe you can wash it off in the kitchen sink." Samantha's soothing tone eased the pulsing headache but caused Ellie's teeth to grind together. She didn't need anyone trying to babysit her.

She needed a prank that Jarrad would never forget. His was clever. He'd set the bar. Now she had to leap over it and put it so high he'd never outdo her. It was no more than he deserved after pranking Connor and now her.

Her arms sparkled in the light. Ellie caught a laugh as it escaped. Her snort blasted louder than an elephant's trumpet. Samantha grinned, and Ellie let loose. She wasn't mad so much as stunned. He'd gotten her good.

"This is what life with Jarrad would be like." Ellie sobered as she spoke the words. She looked at Samantha and sighed. "An endless parade of pranks and jokes. Never being serious."

"I thought you were having fun."

"I was." Ellie turned her arms and battled the mixture of laughter and tears. "But I like serious too. I'm not the type of person who can feel okay with the constant worry of when the next prank will happen. Being afraid of what I'll find in the bed or getting startled every time I open a canister out of fear of what's inside. That isn't me."

Samantha patted Ellie's shoulder. "I'd hug you, but I don't want glitter on me." She brushed specks of glitter from Ellie's hair and pushed her mouth to the side. "Is that why you like Connor? He's serious all the time."

"Maybe." Though Connor had his faults too. A bit too serious. Good grief. Was she being too dramatic or asking for too much? "I want a balance of fun and laughter but someone who's also not afraid to sit down and have a serious conversation."

"I can't answer that for you. Jarrad's a good guy. So is Connor. Maybe we can figure out a way to fuse them together into the perfect-for-Ellie guy."

If only.

Samantha reached for a roll of packing tape. "I have an idea. Let's use tape to get the glitter off you. It's either that or brush you with the broom."

Ellie curled her nose. She knew where that broom had been the last few days. "Tape it is. Try not to pull out all my hair."

"Oh, honey, I'm not touching that. You'll need a dozen showers, and you'll probably still sparkle like Edward."

A groan worked its way up. "First a mad fairy and now a sparkly vampire. What kind of books have you been reading?"

"The best kind." Samantha lifted a shoulder and pulled out a strip of tape. "And I might have an idea for a revenge prank."

"We're going to kidnap Jarrad and strap him to a tree in his underwear using a roll of tape?"

Samantha's laugh eased the tightness in Ellie's chest. Her cousin gave an approving nod. "That would pay him back for stealing your bra, but no." As she ran the tape over Ellie's shirt and shorts, she explained her plan.

With each word, Ellie's grin stretched wider until her cheeks ached from smiling. Revenge. What a sweet way to send a message.

Chapter Fifteen

JARRAD'S PHONE RANG for the twentieth time in ten minutes. He swiped to ignore the call. Unknown number. He wasn't falling for that again. The first time he'd thought it was a fluke. The second time, he began to believe someone hated him. After that, he stopped answering. His voice mail filled up. No sense deleting them just for more to take up space.

The question he wanted answered: Who. Who did this to him? And why? Okay, he wanted all the questions answered.

Shoving his way through the door of Rose Resort, Jarrad paused inside the lobby. Nathan waited with a smirk and folded arms. "You've done it this time."

"What?" Jarrad eyed the empty lobby.

"That glitter bomb backfired."

Oh. That. He bit back a grin. The video feed was priceless. He'd seen every moment of Ellie's reaction. It cut off once she backed out of the frame. He'd like to have been able to hear her, but from the look on her face, not much talking happened. "Backfired?" It had gone exactly as planned.

Nathan pulled his phone from his pocket and flipped it around for Jarrad to see. A billboard filled the screen. A billboard with a picture of Jarrad and a tagline: Who you gonna call? With his phone number plastered across the bottom.

"No way." His phone rang again as though to mock the words. Jarrad groaned and turned the sound off. "Who? Ellie."

Nathan nodded and grinned. "Payback. Ellie decided on a take-no-prisoners approach. She was furious after spending hours cleaning up all that glitter. Nice prank, by the way. One of your best yet."

"I didn't mean to make her mad." She'd not looked mad in the video. Shocked. But not mad. "It was harmless."

Nathan shrugged. "Looks like you have a problem to solve. End the pranks is my recommendation." He moved to the front door and strode outside.

No way. "I have a better idea." If she wanted to play, he'd show her who owned this game. He spun away from Nathan. Time to step up the stakes.

Ellie left the kitchen and strolled toward the storage closet. She must be working on something at the resort today. An idea jumped and begged for attention. Jarrad didn't take time to consider, he ran around the corner and dialed the resort phone.

A shrill ring brought Ellie out of the closet and to the desk.

Jarrad ran down the hall and eased into the closet. A quick twist of his wrist and the lightbulb came loose in his hand. He dropped it onto a shelf and crouched behind a box.

Ellie's steps gave her away as she approached the room. Quick thumps spoke of annoyance and her hissed breath caused him to smile. She stepped into the closet.

Jarrad pushed the door shut with his hand while remaining hidden in shadows. The door creaked but swung closed and latched. He jammed a screwdriver into the crack between the door and the frame, holding it shut.

To his right, Ellie fumbled in the dark. The light switch clicked. Her breaths quickened and the scrape of her shoes on the floor grew loud. She stumbled over a box and sent it tumbling down beside him.

Ellie jiggled the doorknob. "Mom. I'm stuck in the closet." She twisted the knob again and let out a howl when it turned but the door didn't open.

A shaft of light around the door gave Jarrad enough light to see Ellie's hands clawing at the door. "Mom!" She pounded a fist on the wood. "Why is it hot in here?" Her voice dropped to a mumble.

He shifted, and his foot scraped the floor.

"Who's here?" Ellie panted and pressed her back to the door. "Jarrad? Are you in here?" She shivered and scooted to the left. "If you did this, you better come out, or I'll...I'll..."

"What? You'll tell your daddy?" He popped up from behind the boxes and leaned close enough that his breath caressed her cheek.

She screamed and slapped at him. "Don't do that."

He reached out and put a hand on her shoulder.

Ellie leaped away and smacked at his hand. "I said don't. Turn on the light and let me out of here." Her breathing turned erratic, each gasp bringing a wheezing sound into the room.

"I'm trying to, but I need you to move." He plucked the light from the shelf and twisted it back into the socket. Yellow light bloomed, highlighting Ellie's sallow cheeks and sweat trickling down her neck. "What's wrong?"

"Claustrophobic." She held both hands to her throat and sucked in a gasp of air. "Can't breathe. Get me out of here. This isn't funny."

He pulled the screwdriver from the frame and swung the door open.

Ellie rushed out and dropped her hands to her knees. Bent at the waist, she gulped air like a starving person brought to a buffet.

He risked putting a hand on her back. "Hey, are you okay?"

"I will be. Just. Need a minute."

"Ellie, I'm sorry. I didn't know."

She waved a shaking hand. "Tim convinced me to get into the toy box when I was six. He sat on the lid and wouldn't let me out till Mom found him. Been this way ever since." With one last pull of oxygen, she straightened and glared at him.

He palmed the back of his neck and groaned. "Man, I've really sunk to the bottom of the barrel if I'm pulling tricks like Tim the Tool." He grimaced and cleared his throat. "Sorry. He's your brother, but he's a jerk most of the time."

Ellie ran a hand over her red cheeks and smoothed her hair. "Nathan took the lion's share of good genes. Not sure what happened with Tim."

He smiled, but her lips thinned. He'd messed up. Big time.

"That was the stupidest thing you've ever done. No more pranks. Okay? It's too much."

"You started it."

"Do you hear yourself?" Ellie planted her hands on her hips and breathed so hard through her nose that her nostrils quivered. "How old are you? This isn't a preschool. We're work colleagues. Let's keep it at that." She crossed her arms over her chest and shivered. "Let's keep the peace and stay out of each other's way. I think it's best if you don't help me with the bakery anymore."

His world collapsed into itself, a black hole of emptiness sucking away the peace and happiness he'd found here on Nantucket. "You don't want my help? At all?"

"I think that's best."

Fine. If that's what she wanted. Jarrad's jaw tightened. How old are you? Her words rang over and over, a rushing that never stopped. His dad asked the same question when Jarrad did something unexpected. Like let a couple keep their house instead of demanding an inspection that would force them out onto the street. He pushed the inadequacy down deep where Ellie wouldn't see it written across his face and strode away. He'd wanted to get closer to her and prove he'd grown up. Instead he proved the opposite. He was still that teenage boy doing all the wrong things to get attention from a girl he liked. Some things never changed.

Until now.

He retreated into his parents' unit and turned his anger into energy. If he couldn't do right by Ellie, he could at least scrub floors and wash counters until he didn't feel like a complete failure. Remorse dug its claws in and pricked his heart. He'd not meant to frighten Ellie. Connect with her. Show her how well they worked together. But never push her away. Why did he always have to mess things up?

ELLIE WIPED TEARS FROM her eyes and hugged her middle. Sending Jarrad away hurt like nothing she'd felt before. It had to be done. His childish antics pushed too hard against her concept of serenity. She looked over her shoulder at the closet and shuddered. Despite the light now illuminating the interior, a darkness seemed to hover in the corners, waiting for her step back inside.

She gave Jarrad time to leave the building before she crept back to the front desk and flopped into her chair.

"What'd you do to him?" Nathan popped his head into the lobby, letting in a gust of rose-scented air. He took a long look at her and walked to her side. "This can't be good. Did he hurt you? Do I need to beat him up?"

"What is the deal with boys acting like they're five when they're twenty-five. Or older." She gave Nathan a pointed glance that he shrugged off.

"That whole 'boys will be boys' thing only goes so far. When someone we love is hurt, we need to fix it. By any means necessary." He dropped into a matching chair and swiveled to face her. His hands tightened on the chair arms. "What happened?"

Ellie unloaded the whole story in one long stuttering diatribe. Nathan listened without interrupting and except for the occasional nod, Ellie would wonder if he even heard her words.

When she finished, he pushed away from the desk and spun in lazy circles. "Tell me the truth. Is any of that worth losing your friendship over."

She gaped at her brother. "You think I'm overreacting?"

"About the closet, no. But, in his defense, he didn't know. If he'd asked me about it, I would have told him. Do you think he would have intentionally pulled that prank if he knew about your claustrophobia?"

"No." She answered without thinking, but she knew it was true. Jarrad might be immature, but he would never hurt her. "I just don't think the two of us work as a couple." Wait. Couple? When did she start thinking about Jarrad as a possible relationship? He'd worked his way under her defenses, and she never saw him coming. Which made this worse. A glitter bomb she could handle. Not what he did today. Even Nathan admitted it was too much.

"You admit you have feelings for him." Nathan spun and nodded. "That's something, at least. I thought we'd continue going in circles for another half hour before you brought it up."

"It'll never work. I don't trust him."

"Do what you have to do, Ellie." Nathan pushed forward and slid his feet on the floor until the chair stopped turning. He ended face to face with her. "Make sure you're doing it for the right reasons. Don't push Jarrad aside because your feelings scare you."

"I'm not." Again, the words came out of their own accord, but this time, she tasted the hint of a lie in the outburst. The last effects of claustrophobia cleared from her head and her fingers stopped trembling. She locked eyes with her brother. "We're better off as friends." The ache in her chest stated otherwise. Ellie pushed it down, down, down, until it became tolerable. She wanted safety and security. Not surprises and uncertainty. And above all, she wanted her bakery. A relationship with either man forced her to split her attention, a fact brought home by the ping of Connor's text asking if she wanted to go out later.

Nathan lifted an eyebrow at the expulsion of air she released while typing out a quick response that she had work to do. Mainly, cleaning up the last of the glitter and setting out the decor. She ignored Nathan and asked Connor if he wanted to join her at the building.

His response was a lukewarm "I guess" that had Ellie rolling her eyes and leaning into the comfort of her chair.

Jarrad would have jumped at the chance. Stop comparing them. Her silent admonishment caused her hands to clench. She drew the resort's books closer and reached for a pencil. The least she could do was finish her work before she took off for the day. Her parents were still looking for a replacement. One woman had potential, but a final decision had yet to be made. Ellie feared they were stalling, either in hopes of her changing her mind or in fear that she'd flop, and the business would never open or fail right away.

Not happening.

Nathan pulled the pencil from her hand and nudged her aside. "Go. Take a walk on the beach or something. You're wearing me out with all the sighing."

"I'm not sighing."

"You want me to prove it to you?" Nathan tapped his phone screen and a video of Ellie popped up. Every other breath, she made a sound and her shoulders lifted to her ears.

Heat touched her cheeks. "Delete that. Right now." She snatched the phone from him and erased the embarrassing footage. "You didn't send it to anyone, did you?"

"Have you forgotten which twin you're talking to? I'm the good one, remember." He tweaked her nose and rose, pulling her up by the arm as he went. "Get out of here. I'll take care of the receipts."

"I should. It's my job."

"Not for long. You're moving on to your dream job. Let it go. Do something fun and forget all this nonsense. Go clear your head or whatever it is women do when they're stressed and don't know what to do with themselves." He shrugged when she glared. "What? I don't know anything about women. Cut me some slack."

The honesty in his voice brought a smile. He wasn't exaggerating. Where Tim thought he knew what every woman wanted, Nathan tended more toward the strong, silent type who remained clueless and had no qualms about admitting his weaknesses. She gave him a quick hug. "Thanks. You're my favorite brother."

"I better be." He grinned and shooed her away.

Ellie stepped into the afternoon light and let the scent of roses fill her up. How could anyone be sad when the world smelled of roses? She turned away from the long row of houses, where she risked running into Jarrad, and took the winding path down to the beach. Her shoes hit the sand with a soft plop and her toes wiggled into the warm granules. Nothing helped her figure out life like a serene walk on the beach as the sun lowered to the horizon. A new day tomorrow. New opportunities. New decisions to make. Everything was made new. Everything except her words to Jarrad. Words she meant but still regretted.

She'd spoke out of fear but the truth in them lingered, a weight chained to her limbs that made each step harder than the last.

Letting him go would be hard but necessary.

Her phone pinged and her heart skipped. Disappointment all but knocked her to her knees when Connor's name came up on the screen instead of Jarrad's. Why would Jarrad bother to message her? He'd apologized and she pushed him away.

End of story.

A story with Connor was beginning. A new chapter in her life divided as unevenly as a ripped page. She trusted in Connor's maturity to help her. He understood what she wanted and needed with opening her own business.

Chapter Sixteen

JARRAD DELIVERED THE plate of food, sliding it onto the table and turning away. He made it two steps before a man's voice pulled him around.

"I think this is the wrong order."

Jarrad glanced at the food and grunted. "You didn't order chicken Marsala?"

The man shook his head. His throat bobbed on a swallow. Thin and well-groomed, he reminded Jarrad of his dad. This gentleman gifted Jarrad with a smile. "It looks wonderful, though. Perhaps I'll try it."

"I can get your order. It's no problem." It wouldn't be the first order he'd messed up tonight. His brain resembled scrambled eggs. Nothing wanted to stay in place. Thoughts scattered. Memories of Ellie were the only thing that stuck around and held any hope or happiness. Even thoughts of being closer to opening his own place had lost their appeal when he lost Ellie.

All because he'd acted like an immature idiot and locked her in a closet.

Two weeks and he still wasn't over it.

Neither was Ellie, if her silence was any indication.

"Are you kidding?" The man chewed a second bite, then swallowed. "This is the best thing I've ever eaten here."

Lucky mistake. Jarrad forced out a smile though his heart had lost any desire to be happy the day he walked away from Ellie.

It's for the best. You don't want to be stuck with someone who doesn't know how to take a joke. No matter how many times he said it, he didn't believe himself.

He took a step back from the table. "Thank you for being so generous." Not many would let a mistake like that slide, and this man even seemed pleased with the results.

"I've learned that it's often best to roll with the punches. You can't control life, so why bother trying." He took another bite and gave an appreciative nod of his head while patting his stomach. "Some of life's best moments are the unexpected ones."

"I know someone who would disagree with you." Ellie's face flashed into Jarrad's mind. Her pale cheeks and panting breath as she attempted to escape the closet. That moment hadn't been appreciated.

"Well not everything works out as well as this." He hefted his fork.

At the next table, a woman lifted her hand, signaling for Jarrad. He cut down a groan before it slipped out. "I should get back to work. Enjoy your meal."

"Oh, I plan on it."

Jarrad hurried to the woman's side. "How can I help you?"

She sent a harried glance over his name tag and drummed her fingertips on the table. "I'm still waiting on my food, Jarratt. It's been twenty minutes."

"It's Jarrad. I'd be happy to check on your food for you. Give me just a moment." He hurried away before she could say anything else. The clatter of voices in the dining area helped drown out her nasally tone if she did attempt to call him back. He could say with all honesty he never heard her. She wasn't even his table to worry about, but it was good manners for him to offer assistance.

Once in the kitchen, he caught Connor's attention. "Woman at table eight wants to know where her food is."

"There." Connor pointed his spatula at one of the new cooks.

A cook Connor brought in to take Jarrad's place in the kitchen while he continued to bus tables instead of using his degree. Heat scorched the back of Jarrad's neck. He kept his temper in check by the thinnest shred and turned on his heel to find Leslie coming through the doors. Table eight was her territory. "Eight's getting hangry." He passed Leslie and retreated to a dim corner where he could breathe without the smell of garlic and onion drawing him deeper into the rush of anger.

Cooks called out to each other as they synced each order and streamlined the kitchen. He longed to be part of that noise and rhythm. Why did Connor keep him out of the kitchen? He never crossed paths with Ellie anymore, so why the continued punishment? He knew what it meant to Jarrad to be part of the line.

A sharp poke on the back of his neck sent him spinning. He'd leaned against Ellie's corner of the kitchen on accident. Or maybe it was intentional. He didn't know anymore. The edge of one of those ridiculous stickers she'd plastered here over a month ago had begun to curl in the constant heat and steam of the kitchen. He rubbed the back of his neck where it had pricked him. Even now he couldn't escape her.

"Order for table eleven." Connor shouted over the melee.

Eleven was Jarrad's table. One of them.

He took the plate and carried it to the waiting patron, then retreated back to the kitchen. What was he doing here? Working a job he despised. Two, really. The cleaning thing wasn't too bad, but he came to Nantucket to find happiness. He'd grasped it with both hands and hauled it close where he planned to never let go.

And in one swoop, he tossed it overboard faster than a lobsterman with a too-small crustacean. Maybe he should go back. Find his way in the real estate world and make his parents happy.

Make them happy while he remained miserable.

Stay on Nantucket and endure a different type of misery.

The scent of cherry blossoms drifted on a wave of sugary delight, and Jarrad was hauled from his thoughts. Ellie wore that fragrance. And she always smelled of sugar. Like cherries dipped in cotton candy. Light and sweet and addictive.

The woman of his dreams. She strode through the kitchen, a woman on a mission, and paused by Connor's side. They carried on a rushed conversation. Ellie's lips moved a mile a minute as her hands gestured at the pantry, the stove, and then at the cooks filling the kitchen. Her brow furrowed at Connor's reply and she chewed on her bottom lip. Dark circles showed she'd been working hard with little sleep.

What had been an ache turned into an inferno.

ELLIE COULD FEEL JARRAD'S eyes on her. She forced her attention to stay with Connor, who continued shaking his head and swirling butter in the cast iron skillet. He dropped a sirloin steak into the butter. The sizzle mixed with the scent of cooking beef paused Ellie mid-sentence. Her stomach gave a gurgle, reminding her she'd neglected her lunch. Again.

A splash of red drew her attention to the shelf beside Connor's stove. The joke book she'd given Jarrad hid under one of Connor's recipes. She recognized the bright neon and the bent pages she'd marked when she read through the book before giving it to Jarrad. Why did Connor have it? Did Jarrad give it to him after their fight?

"I'm heading back." She searched for Jarrad without turning her head and found him lounging by her flour container.

From the corner of her eye, she lacked the ability to see his expression, but tension drew his shoulders up despite the relaxed posture. He shifted and touched one of her labels with his thumb. He might as well have stroked her cheek for the tenderness in the motion. Her breath caught. How did he get under her skin without even coming near?

"I'll try and come by later, but it's a busy night and I need to get ahead for tomorrow." Connor flipped the steak, then spooned butter over the top. "You'll understand once you have an entire kitchen under your command." He kissed her cheek before pulling away and dropping the steak onto a plate. "Order table fifteen." His voice caused half the kitchen to jerk in his direction as though he was a puppet master and they his marionettes.

How much was she willing to sacrifice for a well-run kitchen? She wanted efficiency but also for her employees to enjoy their work. Ellie took in the faces of the people surrounding her. Most were drawn into frowns that she'd always associated with the stress of the kitchen. Cooking was hot, thankless work, but when you loved it and worked with the right team, it made all the difference.

No one here smiled. They shouted back to Connor when he asked a question, but otherwise the only noise came from the radio and the food as it cooked.

Ellie left the kitchen with her mind in turmoil. She needed to think, to evaluate what she'd seen and misunderstood all these years.

"Ellie." Connor jogged after her, his chef's coat spotless even after hours of cooking. "I'll still see you in the morning for your shift."

She bobbed her head. "Sure." One more week and she'd be manning her own kitchen with her two employees. Surely they could have fun and laugh while kneading dough and drizzling icing. It had to be easier than what Connor encountered every day. "Why isn't Jarrad cooking?" The question had been on her mind since he told her about his degree. He should be second after Connor. A sous chef. No one else in the kitchen had the qualifications. "If you gave him the sous chef position, you could work less and enjoy some time off."

"Jarrad isn't ready to be a sous chef. He's too immature. You said it yourself. Besides. I don't want time off." Connor's expression twisted. He picked at the hair net. "I like my work. It's the most important thing in my life."

Ellie's head ricocheted and her body followed her in a backward step. "Excuse me? Why did you ask me out on dates and take me sailing if you never intended it to turn into a relationship?"

"Work will always come first for me. You knew that. I thought you felt the same way. I expect no less from you when you open your bakery.

You want to be a success, so you have to put in the hours. It won't fall in your lap." Connor gave her a look that made Ellie wonder if he'd ever been in love before. Obviously the answer was no. Loving work was one thing but this bordered on obsession. A workaholic who would sacrifice family for the job.

She took another step back. "I'm glad we cleared that up. Don't bother coming by tonight. I don't need your help." She'd rather work alone than be around him right now. Let him idolize his job and feel like no one else could do what he did.

Connor let her go.

And it didn't hurt. Her breath came easier with each step away from the Club Car. One week until Sweet by Design opened its doors, and she became master of her own kitchen.

Ellie took her time strolling the streets between the Club Car and her bakery. A few blocks separated her from Jarrad and Connor. Feet that might as well be an ocean. Couples held hands, meandering down the cobblestone and pausing to point out this or that in the shop windows. Light spilled out of the long row of buildings and splashed over her feet. Laughter caught the wind and danced amid the chatter and soft words. Her shoulders rolled forward as though the weight of losing Jarrad weighed too much. A breath escaped in a half-laugh, but a sob lodged in her throat. She missed Jarrad. His laugh and the way he always had a way of making her feel special even while she saw the next prank building in his eyes.

She needed a prank right about now.

Her stride faltered.

She wanted to laugh and feel special at the same time.

A ring sent her heart thumping against her ribs. Ellie checked her phone. Tim.

"What's wrong?"

Tim's dark laugh skittered into the night to tangle with the shadows.

Ellie shivered as those same shadows wrapped around her. She moved back into the light cast from The Coffee Grind and gripped her phone tighter. "Tim?"

"Can't a brother call his sister without her assuming something is wrong?"

"If Nathan was the one calling, sure. But not you. I haven't talked to you since Katrina's wedding. And then it was only to scold you for being mean to Lauren."

"Ah, Lauren. How is my ex-wife?"

"Happy. Now. What do you want?" Ellie looked up and down the street, waiting for her menace of a brother to pop out like a maniacal jack-in-the-box.

"Mom called. You really opening a bakery?"

"Why do you want to know?"

"Such attitude." His dry tone cut deep. "I just wanted to congratulate you. When's the big day? I might pop in and say hi. Stir up some business for my baby sister."

"I don't need your kind of business, Tim. You'll have people throwing punches in the middle of my dining room." She closed her eyes as the mental images flashed by. Tim had one mode: jerk. And people reacted accordingly.

"Aw. I'm not that bad."

"Yes, you are. Thank you for the offer, but please don't come. It's the thought that counts, or whatever." Ellie took the step into the dark alley and trotted to the beacon of light shining from her bakery window. Hers. The bright logo of a lighthouse-shaped cupcake proclaimed it to be true.

Tim continued muttering into the phone.

"Bye, Tim." Ellie ended the call and ran the rest of the way. "Wow."

"Not a bad job, if I do say so myself." Jim, the man Jarrad hired for the window stencil wiped his hands on a dirty towel that he shoved into his back pocket. "One of my favorites so far. And I've done a lot of logos. When you opening? I'll be around for a few more days. Wouldn't mind having a cupcake on opening day."

The crack in her heart took another beating. Opening day. She pushed past the lump in her throat. "A week from tomorrow. Saturday morning we'll have a grand opening starting at seven a.m."

"I'll be here." He ran a calloused hand over the logo like it was something precious.

"If you have a card, I'd love to keep it on the counter to help promote your business." She scanned the logo and the first real smile in days pulled at her lips. "You just made this real for me. Thank you."

"It was my pleasure." He took a battered card from his shirt pocket and passed it to her before he shook her hand, climbed into his truck, and rolled away.

Ellie traced the curls and whirls that made up the words climbing up the lighthouse. All the work. All the time spent, and the uneasy nights were coming together into a final moment. Her dream business was in front of her, and all she wanted was to call Jarrad and have him live the moment with her.

Chapter Seventeen

ELLIE STIRRED THE POT of milk and sprinkled yeast at the same time. The aroma soothed her with its familiarity. Her first day in her bakery kitchen. Tomorrow was her grand opening. She'd spent a week working on organizing the kitchen and putting everything within easy reach for recipes.

"What next?" Julie, Ellie's head baker, peered over Ellie's shoulder and scrunched her nose. "Smells funny. Is it supposed to smell like that?"

"That's the yeast. What's next on the recipe?" Ellie knew it by heart, but this was Julie's last chance to have Ellie by her side. She stepped away from the pot and waved Julie closer. "Take over from here. I'll watch."

Julie pressed her lips together but took control of the spoon. "I need flour."

Ellie waited. The container sat in front of Julie, the black on white label sending Ellie crashing back to the moment months ago in Connor's kitchen when she'd been furious with Jarrad. The crack in her heart widened into a chasm. She'd learned to live with the constant pain of missing him.

Breathing deeply through her nose, Julie pulled the flour container close and scooped in eight level cups. Her brown hair bobbed with each one. She stirred until the dough came together, then beamed a megawatt smile. "Now we wait and let it rise."

"How long do we wait?"

"An hour." Julie tossed a towel over the pot to trap heat and dusted off her hands. "I do this every morning?"

"Yep."

"What if I need you for something?"

"You have my number. And I'll be coming in every morning to check on you until you're comfortable doing it on your own." And until Ellie felt comfortable leaving the woman alone.

Julie stretched her shoulders and rolled her head side to side. "What are we making next?"

"Scones." Ellie started to grab her recipe book. The slot in the cabinet was empty. "Have you seen my recipe book?"

"I thought that was it." Julie pointed at the pink and yellow box where most of Ellie's recipe cards had found a home over the years.

Oh no. She'd left it at the Club Car. "I have to run out. I'll be back before the next step."

"No rush." Julie waved her away. "The next part is easy. I could do that in my sleep."

Kneading dough. Yeah, she knew the feeling. She'd had dreams where bowls of dough danced and stretched themselves into miraculous loaves that never ran out when she first started working with Connor. Hazard of the job.

She left Julie lounging and scrolling through her phone. The early morning haze held Nantucket hostage, suspended in time until the sun dared lift over the water and wake their little world. Building after building passed. White. Then brown until she ducked around the corner and to the back of the restaurant. Connor opened the door when she knocked. He took her in from head to toe. "Ellie."

"I forgot my recipe book."

"I'll get it for you." He disappeared into the kitchen without a backward glance.

So this was what they were relegated to? Why the sudden shift and the feeling of animosity burning between them?

Connor shoved the book through a crack in the door.

"What's your problem?" Maybe she should be nicer. She wanted his business, but the decision was only partly in his hands. David had the final say, and he'd already signed an agreement offering Ellie a decent price for her bread. She pushed the anger from her expression and attempted to rein in the emotions that served no purpose when dealing with Connor.

He stepped into the alley and tossed an eggshell into the recycle bin. "I thought we understood each other. That our dates were leading us somewhere official. We're the same. Serious and work oriented. I tried acting more like Jarrad when I saw you seemed to prefer a casual approach, but it felt wrong. This is who I am. I decided I can't change that."

"Excuse me? When did you act like Jarrad?"

"When I pretended to let the air out of my tires. I saw it in that prank book he left in the kitchen. It didn't work out like I planned, but we had a nice time. You liked my stories. What happened?" Genuine confusion crossed his face.

"You did that?" An abyss developed at the bottom of the chasm where a longing for Jarrad continued to throb. She'd acted three kinds of a fool by pranking Jarrad and then getting mad when he repaid her. Her actions required an apology. She'd allowed herself to put it off. No more.

Connor angled his head to the side. "You didn't get it or find it funny, so I let it go. It doesn't work trying to be someone else."

"No, it doesn't." She had to find Jarrad. Right now. Or as soon as possible. Julie needed her to return soon. Ellie turned away from Connor, her heart stretching its limits between breaking and hoping that they might overcome the past yet again. She wanted her bakery. But she wanted to share it with Jarrad. She ran back to the bakery to check on Julie.

Tossing the recipe book on the counter she and Jarrad spent hours painting, Ellie took in the building. Everywhere she looked, she saw Jarrad. His presence tapped her shoulder at the sight of a fleck of glitter stuck in a crack in the hardwood floor. His laugh tickled her thoughts when she ran her hand over the shelving.

That night of painting with him held more emotion than she'd known possible. She wanted that back. The carefree camaraderie and feeling of belonging with someone who knew how to dream.

How to show him? Saying the words was one thing, but she needed to make a statement. Something he'd understand came from her heart and spoke to his in a way he couldn't deny.

She ran every movie he'd ever mentioned through a reel in her head. None of them gave her any ideas. What if...

"You okay?" Julie flipped through the recipe book and watched Ellie from the corner of her eye.

Not in the least. "Thinking." Ellie spun in a circle. This building, the business, she owed it to Jarrad. Even when she told him to back off and leave her alone, he lingered in every second she spent here. "Keep working the bread. I have something to take care of."

"You got it, boss." Julie tapped her forehead in a mini salute. "I think I can handle the scones too. Mind if I give them a try?"

"Knock yourself out." Incentive. Hiring Julie had been the right choice. She might be young, but she had a good work ethic. Ellie gathered up a stack of cardboard boxes and the roll of tape. Holding the supplies tight to her chest, she set out for her cottage at a trot. Each pounding step brought her idea to life. She plotted out what she wanted to say and imagined Jarrad's reaction. Either he'd understand, or he wouldn't. She had no choice but to try.

Her breath caught, a searing pain lodging deep in her left side that forced her to slow to a walk. Hints of pink and purple bruised the horizon. She forged ahead without stopping to watch the breaking of dawn. If this worked out, every sunrise from this point on would have new meaning.

JARRAD CONSIDERED IGNORING the pounding on his front door. Exhaustion pulled on his eyelids and each gritty blink felt like grains of sand scouring his eyes. What could possibly be worth ruining the first few hours of sleep he'd managed to catch since the day he locked Ellie in that closet?

Thinking of that day hurt too much, so he locked it away. He'd apologized. Ellie obviously didn't accept. She continued to avoid him and spend her time with Connor. Images of her standing by Connor's side in the kitchen burned bright in his subconscious. He growled and shook his head, attempting to knock the pictures loose.

His door rattled again.

"I'm coming." His voice came out a gruff bellow and the thudding stopped. Five more minutes of sleep, then he'd answer the door. He closed his eyes, but they popped right back open. Curiosity prodded him from the bed and had his hand reaching for a shirt as he padded toward the front door.

He jerked it open with a grumble, the shirt still wadded in his hand. "What?"

Ellie.

The world narrowed to her. Just Ellie and the sudden tension banding his chest.

She wore ripped jeans and a blue tank top. Flour dotted her nose, telling him she'd been baking this morning. A hint of sugar and honey shot into his nose. He fought the urge to breath deep enough to take that scent to the center of his being and hold it there forever.

He focused on her face. She looked him up and down, pausing for a beat on his bare chest before looking into his eyes and swallowing hard. Curls framed her face, the wild kind that he loved so much it hurt. His hands clenched as the urge to reach out and tug one slammed into his gut.

Ellie held a piece of cardboard behind her back. She shifted left to right, and the silence between them stretched to the point of breaking his mind into a thousand pieces. He opened his mouth, intending to ask her why she'd interrupted his sleep at dawn.

Before he could get the words out, she held a finger to her lips and tapped her phone. He recognized the soundtrack for *The Princess Bride* right away. Ellie straightened her shoulders and brought the cardboard to her chest.

Jarrad read the first card silently.

"I once said you would never be a Wesley."

She grimaced and dropped the card, revealing a second.

"The truth is, I was afraid of how you made me feel."

The band around his chest tightened. He looked up.

Ellie shook her head and tapped the cardboard while tears gathered in her eyes.

Cardboard hit the ground, revealing the next card.

"Like Buttercup, I thought I knew what I wanted."

He took a step forward. Ellie took one back and let go of the board.

"To me, you are perfect."

And the next.

"And I'm sorry."

His heart jackhammered, thudding his ribs in painful bursts.

Tears dripped from her chin. Ellie let them fall as though proud to show him the brokenness inside her own heart. She gathered up the cardboard and ended the music.

"Now you know." Her voice shattered the silence. She spun away in a single move and burst into a run.

Jarrad took off after her. "Ellie, wait."

She ran like the wind, darting down the path and churning sand.

He followed as fast as he could but lost sight of her at the edge of town. Most likely she was headed to her bakery. He could follow and hope to find her there.

Sand pelted his chest as a rush of wind raced up the beach. He should put a shirt on before going into town. Jarrad glanced down, but his hand was empty. He'd dropped or thrown the shirt at some point but had no memory of the action. Only Ellie.

What did her cards mean?

He knew the scene she recreated from *Love, Actually*. That scene was about a man in love with his best friend's wife. What was Ellie trying to say? She loved him? Why not say it straight out?

The whole thing might be another prank. Doubtful. Not after how the last one turned out. He backtracked and found his shirt in the sand where the path curved around a thick patch of grass. After shaking out the sand, he trudged the rest of the way home, planning the entire time.

Ellie's gesture fanned the flame that first sparked upon his return to Nantucket.

She forgave him. Maybe even wanted a second chance. He'd know for certain after tomorrow, when she discovered what he'd done even before she appeared on his doorstep.

Chapter Eighteen

OPENING DAY. ELLIE pressed a hand to her stomach to ease the queasiness churning there. It didn't help. She'd spent most of the night pacing her living room and chewing her lip until it was a mess of torn skin that even lipstick couldn't cover. Doubts and fears assailed her at every turn. What if no one showed up?

By 5 a.m. she'd paced herself into a frenzy before breaking down and getting ready to face the day. She showered and changed into her favorite white top and jean capris with a pair of canvas shoes that were both comfortable and functional. Knowing she'd be on her feet all day, if the opening was a success, she fortified her shoes with extra support padding and set out at a brisk walk for the bakery.

Her first sign that something wasn't right came in the form of her brother. Nathan met her at the edge of town, and his face creased into a wide smile. "Happy opening day." He embraced her and hugged tight enough to lift her onto her toes.

"Thanks, but I can't breathe." Ellie patted his shoulders and returned to the ground. She scooped her hair into a quick bun and hurried forward.

Nathan matched her stride.

"What are you doing?"

His arms swung loose by his sides, the epitome of causal grace, her brother. "Walking with you. Not every day your little sister achieves a dream. I'm not missing this."

She encountered her parents next, the two of them holding hands in front of the bakery. They beamed. Mom wiped away a tear and gave Ellie a side hug while still holding Dad's hand. "Congratulations, honey. We're so proud of you."

"Thanks." Why did she feel like she'd be saying that a lot today? She could only hope that might be true. Her throat turned to sandpaper. "Would you like to come inside? I'll start some coffee."

"Better keep it going." Nathan grinned the slow smile of a man with a secret.

Ellie popped her hands onto her hips. "What's that supposed to mean?"

"You haven't seen?"

She shook her head as her thoughts fell into each other. "Seen what?"

Nathan passed her his phone. She winced at the memory of what she'd seen last time he made that action. This time, instead of a video of her humiliating herself, she found Jarrad on the screen. He stood in front of her bakery. The logo shone clear in the mid-day light. When had he filmed this? He stared at the camera and gave the smile that made her heart flutter. "Take a trip with me down the streets of Nantucket and stop by our newest and finest establishment." He brandished one arm over the logo. "Sweet by Design is owned and operated by our very own, Ellie Jones. Come by Saturday morning, take a photo by the logo, and upload it to the bakery's Facebook page. Show your photo to the cashier and receive a free cup of coffee every day for three months. This is a one-day only deal you don't want to miss."

If her jaw dropped any further, she'd have to scoop it off the sidewalk and carry it around. "How? When?" She shook her head. It didn't matter. Jarrad still helped her. After everything.

Nathan took his phone back. "Get ready. It's going to be a busy day. We're here to help."

"All of you? What about the resort?" Ellie wiped her damp palms on her capris. "Is Tim coming?" Her voice squeaked, giving away the fear working to close her throat.

Dad took her hand. "The resort can handle itself for today. This is your day. Tim couldn't make it."

Her heart swelled and tears pricked. Ellie sniffed them away and unlocked the door. "Come in and let's see what happens. We might end up eating our weight in pastries."

"You wouldn't have to twist my arm." Nathan was the first one into the bakery. He paused and took a deep breath. "Best smell ever. If the bakery business goes bust, you could start a perfume company."

Ellie locked the door and strode toward the back. She left the lights off and found her way using only the dim glow from the emergency lights at the back and in the kitchen. "I think Bath and Body Works has the market on burnt sugar smell." Ellie laughed and the tension she'd held all night eased a fraction. Not completely, but enough that she could breathe without feeling like her lungs had forgotten how to function.

Chatter from the front window caught Ellie's attention. Two teenage girls held a phone in front of their faces. The flash of a camera lit up the window. They turned and cupped their hands around their eyes to peer inside.

Ellie waved. "We'll be open in an hour."

They clapped and jumped up and down before pressing the phone against the window, showing off the picture they'd taken and already posted to the community page. "Will we get the deal on the coffee?"

"Yes." Her single word answer was met with more squeals. They moved to the opposite side of the street and settled on a bench, chattering and laughing as they scrolled through the phone.

A lone woman pushing a stroller stopped next and snapped a quick picture. She glanced at her watch, then continued her walk.

The phone in the kitchen rang. Ellie rushed to answer but took a breath to settle her nerves before the quiver in her voice gave her away. "Hello?"

"Is this Sweet by Design?"

"Yes. How can I help you?"

"I run a fish and chips shop down by the pier. Got a promotion for your business and wanted to know if you're interested in partnering with us. When you have time, bring us a sample and a price list. We'll sit down and talk numbers." The voice was gruff in a pleasant way, like the tang of Key Lime pie on a summer day.

Ellie fumbled her way through an answer and scribbled the man's information down on a scrap sheet of paper she'd thought to put by the phone. As soon as she hung up, the phone rang again. She listened to the same spiel from a woman this time and jotted down the name and a time to meet. Sweat gathered in the small of her back. What was happening? She hadn't advertised for company baking like this other than her agreement with the Club Car. Did they have something to do with this?

The two companies alone would keep her busy two days of the week if she landed their business. Ellie lowered the receiver. It hardly touched before the shrill ring sounded again. "I'll take care of that." Mom took the phone and pencil from Ellie. "You go handle the front. Let people see you so they know who they're doing business with. Steve, get me a notebook." She picked up the receiver and answered with a smooth trill that had brought in countless couples to the Rose Resort over the years.

Ellie listened to her mother. The woman knew what she was talking about. Once more, her mouth fell open when she stepped into the dining area. A line stretched all the way along the front of the building. People nodded and smiled and excused themselves to maneuver in front of the logo for a picture.

"I don't understand." Ellie rocked her head while pressing her palms to her temples. "This is more than I ever expected."

Nathan chortled from his spot at a table near the back corner. "All of Nantucket seems to have shown up for you."

"But why?"

"Because you're part of the community. They believe in you. We all do." He paused.

The air conditioning chugged, pushing out drafts of cool air to chill her skin. His silence rattled her. Nathan never held back from telling her the truth. She edged closer. "What aren't you telling me?"

"There's someone who believes in you even more than the rest of us."

Jarrad. The world stopped turning as everything clicked into place. "There's no way he did all of this overnight. He's been planning for weeks." Why would he do that? Her apology yesterday was the hardest thing she'd ever done. She ran away before finding out if he accepted it, but this was more than acceptance. This was an offering of peace that he put into place long ago.

Don't be mad at him." Nathan spun his phone on the table and focused on the spinning object. He lowered his hands to his lap. Behind him, the dark corners seemed to breathe with a life of their own.

Ellie felt him there. Waiting. "I'm not."

"Good." Jarrad stepped out of the shadows. He looked like she felt. Bags under his eyes and hair a rumpled mess. Had he not slept either?

Her family faded into the background. Ellie pushed the murmur of voices and the sounds of Nantucket into the recesses of her mind and let Jarrad take up all the space available in her mind and vision. She stepped toward him. "You could have told me." Her tone was strained. Not in anger, but in appreciation.

His forehead wrinkled. "You said you weren't mad."

"I'm not." And there she went repeating herself. Words left her as she stared up at Jarrad. "I can't believe you would do all this for me after the terrible things I said to you."

He took her hand and gave a tug.

Ellie let herself be pulled closer to the dark corner where they were hidden from the world, her family, and any prying eyes.

"That stunt yesterday made up for all the hurt feelings."

"I put a lot of thought into that."

His lips quirked upward. "I could tell." He looped an arm around her waist. "I'm sorry for everything. I was jealous of Connor."

Ellie harrumphed and patted his chest. "No worries there. Connor is more concerned with work than me. And I'd be lying if I said I was disappointed. I've missed you from the moment I agreed to that first date with Connor."

"Why's that?" He gave her a look that said he knew but needed to hear the words.

Giving in to that need was the easiest thing she'd ever done. She'd always thought falling in love would be hard. With Jarrad, it was as easy as remembering to breathe. Ellie wrapped her arms around his waist and rested her cheek against his chest. "Because he wasn't you."

She stood on tiptoes, bringing them eye to eye.

Jarrad's gaze dropped to her lips. He tipped closer, eyes questioning.

Ellie ran her hands up his back, enjoying the way his shirt bunched under her fingers.

He touched his lips to hers, a butterfly touch that might have been a dream save for the shivery heat cascading down her back. "I love you, Jarrad." Her eyes closed.

If the first touch of his lips was a butterfly, this was the crashing tide rushing over Nantucket's beach. It compelled with irresistible intensity. Jarrad's hands gripped her hips, while Ellie's trailed up his back and into his hair. Every nerve came alive at once in a flash that caused a gasp to escape her lips.

A masculine cough pushed them apart.

Ellie didn't bother hiding her smile or the heat blooming over her face. She lowered her head to Jarrad's chest and let the symphony of his heartbeat lull her home.

HEARING ELLIE'S CONFESSION brought light back to Jarrad's life. After weeks of dull gray, his world came into focus. This was what he'd been missing. Ellie in his arms, her cheek over his heart and his chin on her head as they swayed to music drifting from the kitchen.

The phone continued to ring every few minutes. Margaret's muted voice soothed and cajoled in equal measure. The woman held the companies in the palm of her hand.

Ellie's laughter tickled his neck as she leaned back to look into his eyes. "How did you do all this?"

"Because I love you." Knowing that made the rest a simple matter of picking up the phone. Her success mattered.

Her grip on his waist tightened. Eyes wide and breath frozen with lips open, Ellie stared at him with unflinching awareness. "I didn't know love was a how kind of emotion."

"Didn't you know?" Jarrad kissed the tip of her nose. "Love makes the world go round."

Nathan coughed again. "You two going to separate long enough for Ellie to open her business or not?"

"I like it here." Ellie snuggled closer. "I think I'll stay."

"There's plenty more where that came from." Jarrad squeezed her tight and chuckled. Later. Once the day wound to a close and they could be alone. "Let's get this party started."

"And here I thought you'd whip out a movie line to start us off." Ellie clicked her tongue. "I don't even know who you are anymore."

His chest warmed with a surge of laughter. "Plenty of time for you to figure that out."

Ellie pouted while walking toward the door. She flipped the lock and motioned toward the counter. "Welcome to Sweet by Design. I'm Ellie, the owner. Please come in, browse around, and feel free to ask me any questions you like."

People flooded into the small space. Jarrad pressed his back into a shelf to keep from getting elbowed in the stomach. He recognized a dozen faces, but there were countless others picking up bags of cookies and murmuring over the décor.

Happiness radiated from Ellie. She stood in the middle of the room, gesturing with her hands as she spoke and smiling so wide her cheeks would be sore tomorrow. He planned on making sure that joy never left her face. No matter what he had to do to make her happy, it would be worth the trouble.

It had already been worth it. Every sleepless night, every phone call. Jarrad settled into the background, slipping into the supporting role he hoped to never leave. He'd done it. He'd become Egon to her Janine.

Ellie's hand shot into the air. She waved. "Jarrad, can you come here?"

He'd rather not. Watching her dream blossom into reality made him happy enough.

"Please?"

That did it. He strode across the room, dodging people with each step. "How may I be of service?"

Laughter danced in her eyes. Ellie pursed her lips and rocked on her heels as she nodded her head toward the wall. "Fetch me that pitcher?"

Ah, she was on another *Princess Bride* kick. High on the wall of shelves, a pink pitcher sat nestled in a tall nook. "As you wish." Jarrad inclined his head. Even his hair cooperated with the scene by flopping over his forehead. He shifted, reaching over her head and pulling the pitcher down. Anyone within a dozen feet probably heard his pounding heart.

Ellie gazed up at him. "I have a proposition for you."

"Oh, really?" He cradled the pitcher to his chest, protecting it from the jostling crowd. "I wonder what it could be. I'm rather fond of pink gemstones, so if you're planning to propose you might want to take that into consideration." He winked and trailed his finger down the side of her neck. Her throat bobbed, and she tucked her chin into his wrist.

"While that sounds lovely, I had something different in mind." She took the pitcher from him and passed it to a white-haired lady wearing pink slippers. "Here you go. That's Samantha's latest. A one of a kind."

White curls, still in the rollers, waved as the woman lifted the pitcher to her face and crowed.

Jarrad did a double take. Yep. Pink slippers. With bunny ears. And a pink house robe to match.

The elderly woman grinned at him, showing all gums. "Don't worry, son. I'm not off my cracker. Just didn't feel like getting dressed before daylight." Before he could even close his mouth to respond, she shuffled into the crowd.

"That's Mrs. Melner. You get used to her." Ellie's grin was that of a kid discussing their favorite aunt. "I'd like to hire you. As a marketing and PR manager." She took his arm and turned him in a circle. "All this is because of you. Your hard work and that photo deal you made. Which is going to be a pain in the neck, just so you know. Free coffee for three months. Do you know how much coffee that will be? Katie's going to have a fit."

"How many people have posted?" The challenge started two hours ago. He expected a dozen, maybe two dozen people.

Ellie motioned for Nathan, who hurried their way. "How many?" She asked her brother while she swept the room and continued to smile.

Nathan tapped and ran his thumb down the screen. "Two thousand."

"Wha—"

Ellie poked his chest. "You're on coffee duty. I'll pay you, but that's your job today. You break it, you bought it. Or in this case, you bring the chaos, you take control of it."

Two thousand people had taken their picture with Ellie's logo and posted it online. Jarrad's thought process stalled. He heard nothing but static as Ellie pushed him toward the coffee machine.

"Ellie." Nathan froze and frowned at his screen. He shook his head and swiped. Then swiped again. "You're trending." He flipped the phone around.

Ellie paled and clapped her hands to her cheeks while bright red spots bloomed. "We're going to need more bread. And cookies. And . . . everything." She pushed Jarrad. "Coffee. Please."

He started to walk away.

She caught his arm and pulled him back, planting a quick kiss on his cheek. "Thank you. I love you. Best opening day ever."

Day one in a long line of forever. He didn't even mind. Forever looked pretty good from where he stood.

Ellie hurried away, her curls swinging with each step. She paused to chat with a customer and pointed out a tray of cinnamon rolls that Julie brought out from the kitchen. So they'd convinced her after all. A hungry horde converged on the platter.

Oh yeah. Forever looked better with every second.

Chapter Nineteen

SIX MONTHS LATER...

Ellie draped white fondant over the smallest cake tier, then smoothed out the sides and top before cutting away the excess and moving the small stack to the top of the cake. She took a step back to admire the effect and put the finishing touches on the massive anniversary cake. A trio of red roses across the top to match the bands of red ribbon around each of the three tiers. Her parents' anniversary party was set to begin any minute.

She'd managed to get Mom and Dad to agree to turn the resort over to her and Nathan for the day. The surprise party had been Ellie's idea, but Nathan and Jarrad jumped on board without a struggle.

Jarrad offered the use of his quad and the incentive to visit the lighthouse and enjoy a short vacation. One day. That's all they needed, and all her parents would agree to.

Ellie insisted they'd earned it and with today being their anniversary, she pushed and whined until they gave in. She rubbed her palms together and danced a jig right in the middle of the kitchen.

"Now I see why you didn't want to decorate it at the shop." Jarrad propped a hip on the counter and nudged aside a pastry bag filled with icing. He licked a dot of icing from his finger. "That's delicious. Red velvet and cream cheese icing?"

"Middle layer." She pointed at the largest circle. "Lemon pound cake with vanilla icing, red velvet with cream cheese, then dark chocolate cherry with toasted graham cracker icing."

"You're amazing." Jarrad pulled her into a hug and buried his nose in her hair. "I never get tired of that smell."

"Good, because at this point, I might as well have a sticker on my face that says sugar and spice and everything nice." Ellie breathed in the crispness of his cologne. Here in the kitchen, it was an ambrosia of masculinity amid the heady aroma of baking spices and cake. "I never get tired of this."

His laugh rumbled against her cheek. "Good, because I plan on doing this for the rest of my life."

"I'm on board with that."

It wasn't the first time he'd hinted at marriage. Or at least a forever that included him and her together. She didn't push. There was no need to rush.

"It won't be long and we'll need to plan another party to celebrate Sweet by Design being open a full year. And still as busy as it was that first day." Jarrad rubbed his hands up and down her back. His breath brushed her forehead. "I'm so proud of you."

"Hey, you're doing the heavy lifting. I just bake."

"Right. That's like saying a beach is just a speck of sand."

She lifted a shoulder and snuggled closer, enjoying the closeness of the kitchen and the way his arms instinctively wrapped around her. "We have about five minutes before Mom and Dad get back. That's a two-minute kiss and three minutes of you helping me get this cake into the lobby."

"How about a four-minute kiss and we make Nathan carry the cake?"

"Tempting, but he's been known to trip over his own feet, and I refuse to risk losing my chance to eat a slice of every flavor." Ellie lifted her face to Jarrad. He met her halfway, bringing his lips to hers in that same butterfly kiss that curled her toes with its gentle sweetness.

She leaned in for a second kiss and held on as the rush of emotions carried her away. She never tired of feeling this way, like his kiss, his embrace, the love coursing through her body, could solve any problem. "I love you."

Jarrad tightened his arms. "I love you too." He pulled away and tilted his head toward the door. "I hear guests. We'd better get your cake out there before your parents come back."

Working together, they moved the monstrosity to a rolling cart. Ellie walked ahead and made sure the path was clear for Jarrad, who pushed the cake into the room amid gasps and clapping hands. Ellie mock-bowed and brushed a red streamer from the tabletop so that it fell in a gentle arc against the white tablecloth.

Jarrad moved the cake into place, while Nathan returned the cart to the kitchen.

Samantha hurried over with a platter of fruit. "Sorry I'm late."

"You're right on time." Ellie reassured her when the rumble of an engine cut through the soft chatter. "Is the front clear?"

"Bit late if it wasn't." Samantha smoothed her hands down her front and fluffed her paisley top. "But yes. Most everyone walked. The few who rode bikes or drove hid their transportation behind the vacant units."

Ellie glanced over the crowd of people lining the room. Katrina and her husband huddled together in a corner, giving of newlywed vibes a year after their wedding. Tim frowned into his drink. Her parents' friends were scattered throughout the crowd of family. The open lobby offered no space for anyone to hide.

"They're coming." Nathan flicked a hand from his spot at the window.

The crowd quieted into an expectant hush.

Ellie gripped Jarrad's hand, and he traced gentle circles around her thumb until she relaxed.

Dad opened the door first and held it for Mom without looking inside. Thirty plus years of marriage and she never left the center of his universe. Ellie choked on the lump growing tight in her throat. She glanced up at Jarrad as he squeezed her hand.

"Happy Anniversary!" Half the people in the crowd clapped while the other half blew into party horns. The resulting cacophony had both her parents growing wide eyed. Dad laughed and started shaking hands. Mom grew teary-eyed and patted her cheeks.

Ellie rushed over to hug each of them.

Mom dried her eyes on the napkin Nathan handed her. "Who did this?"

"We all did." Ellie kissed her cheek and hooked her arm around Mom's waist. "We wanted to do something special."

"You did good, kids." Dad's voice boomed from the side of the room. He'd already made his way to the table of food and had a plate half-full.

Samantha hurried past with a platter of glazed donuts. She turned sideways to slip between Nathan and a group of his teacher friends. One man turned and clipped the tray with his elbow. Ellie jolted into action, but it was too late. The platter lifted. Donuts flew into the air. Sam's mouth dropped open, and she lost control of the plate. It clattered to the ground, followed by a spray of donuts. They plopped onto the man's head and icing splattered onto his shirt.

Ellie cringed and ran to gather napkins from the nearest table.

The man responsible for the accident reached for Sam. Concern lined his face. What looked like an apology fell from his lips, but Ellie was too far away to hear the words. She snatched the napkins and ran through the crowd. Samantha took the napkins from Ellie and handed one to the mystery man.

"I had no idea you were behind me. Believe me, I'd never do something like that on purpose." Words continued to pour from his mouth.

Samantha shook her head. "My fault." She began blotting the icing on his shirt. "I'm so sorry." Her cheeks grew pink as the mess smeared further into the cotton, but she seemed determined to keep swiping.

Jarrad hooked Ellie's arm. "Looks like a match made in heaven."

"That's ridiculous." Ellie responded automatically, then took another look at Samantha. Her cousin appeared blissfully unaware of the party going on around her. She nodded and threw her head back in a laugh. Ellie cocked her head and reached out to snag Nathan's arm. "Who's the guy with Sam?"

"New teacher at the high school. He doesn't know many people yet, so I invited him here. Planned on introducing him." Nathan wiggled a finger at the laughing couple. "Looks like Sam beat me to it."

Ellie wished Sam the best. She caught Jarrad's eye and grinned. Love was worth the risk. She'd spent too long pushing him away out of fear that loving him meant giving up the bakery when one had little to do with the other. He supported her every single day. And they thrived because of it. Love and respect went both ways. Working together at the bakery taught her how to love life. Loving Jarrad taught her to love the unexpected gestures and the silliness of the moment.

"I should get more drinks." Nathan took off.

Ellie leaned her head on Jarrad's arm and enjoyed the moment. They'd pulled off another successful event. Mom and Dad laughed and worked through the crowd, bringing smiles everywhere they went.

Family and friends mingled. Many stopped to admire Ellie's cake. Her handiwork had become sought after this past year, mostly thanks to Jarrad and his exceptional marketing skills. He'd discovered he loved the job and though he used his culinary skills in the kitchen anytime he wanted, his desire to work with people brought a newfound joy.

He took her hand and eased toward the door. She squinted and popped her sunglasses on. They were the only people on the porch. Red roses twined up the columns and wrapped around the banisters. Even in mid-afternoon, the aroma saturated the air.

Jarrad backed into a corner and scanned the front walk. Ellie followed his gaze. Her pulse thrummed when he opened his mouth then snapped it shut. He ran a hand through his hair and shoved the other into his pocket. What was going on? He dropped to a knee and pulled out a black box.

Ellie blinked to clear the hallucination. Blinked again when Jarrad still kneeled in front of her. He opened the box with a squeak of the tiny hinges. "Ellie." A diamond glittered.

She ripped off her sunglasses. A pink diamond. He'd bought her a pink diamond.

"I had this whole thing planned. A movie moment, you know. But then I realized, this deserves more than a replica. Though, I did consider dressing in a suit and attempting the whole Sweet Home Alabama scene." He shook his head and kissed the back of her hand. "This felt right. To propose to you in the place where I fell in love."

"I'm assuming you mean you fell in love with me here and not some other woman." Ellie risked the smart remark while smiling. She'd become better at joking over the last year, especially with Jarrad. She leaned down and kissed his forehead. "I feel like I should have a sword so that I could knight you. You're going to need something spectacular if you plan on spending the rest of your life with me."

"Already done." Jarrad winked. "You are spectacular, Ellie Jones, and you'd make me the happiest man in the world if you would be my wife."

"I think I can live with that. I've never been happier than I am when I'm with you."

Jarrad slipped the ring onto her finger and stood while rubbing his knees.

"I'm not making our wedding cake." She shook her curls.

His laugh made her knees go weak. His kiss was sugar sweet and threatened to melt her right then and there. Ellie wrapped her arms around his neck and drew him close enough that their hearts beat together. His palms framed her ribs, the touch scorching to her core. Her worries and fears slipped away under his care and attention. Whatever might come their way, they would face it together.

CHECK OUT THE NEXT release, *Dreaming of Nantucket* by Taryn Daniels

Can a single dad and math teacher take a calculated risk on the adventurous owner of a parasailing business? Meet Samantha Jones, one of the cousins of Nantucket, and root for her as she shows Preston, life is for living—and you can fall in love again on the shores of Nantucket.

Book 3 of The Cousins of Nantucket series. Each novel can be read as a stand-alone and in any order. Characters and setting are connected.

Free Novella

Have you signed up for Taryn's newsletter to get your free copy of *Accidentally Engaged on Nantucket?*

Grab it from www.Payhip.com/TheColabPress or TarynDanielsAuthor.Wordpress.com